The H
Pris

Euan Taylor

First published in Great Britain in 2025

Copyright © Euan Taylor - euantaylorauthor@gmail.com

The right of Euan Taylor to be identified as the Author has been asserted in accordance with the Copyright, Design and Patents Act 1988.

All rights reserved. No part of this publication may be reproduced, stored in a retrieval system, or transmitted in any form or by any means, whether electronic, mechanical, photocopying, recording, or otherwise without the prior written permission of the Publisher. This book may not be lent, resold, hired out, or otherwise disposed of by way of trade in any form of binding or cover other than that in which it is published without the prior written consent of the Publisher.

This is a work of fiction. Names, characters, places, and incidents either are products of the author's imagination or are used fictitiously. Any resemblance to actual persons, living or dead, events, or locales is purely coincidental.

ISBN: 9798316956104

Last Man Standing

As job interviews go, it was a strange one.

I met my first candidate in a cleaning cupboard, temporarily repurposed as a meeting room. Our knees touched as we sat on two plastic chairs facing each other.

Oliver shook my hand firmly, looked me in the eye, and apologised for his nerves.

A good-looking, clean-cut Geordie lad with the physique of a cage fighter, Oliver was surely mistaking his nervousness for total confidence.

He scared the living shit out of me.

"So, I'm looking for an assistant. A point of contact in the office for when I'm not here."

Oliver nodded.

"I need someone who knows the ropes and gets on well with everyone. Have you been here long?"

Oliver leaned back in his seat and shook his head.

"Twelve years, coming up thirteen."

"OK. And are you planning on sticking around much longer?"

"I'm here for life, Sir."

"Please, call me Euan."

"Thank you, Sir."

"So, what does 'life' mean? I mean, you read all sorts of things in the…"

He cut me short.

"Ninety-nine years for double murder."

I tried to play it cool. It was my strategy for surviving in this place. Don't judge. Don't be seen to judge. You don't want to know.

"So you're not going anywhere anytime soon?"

"Between here, my pad, and the gym, you won't need to go too far to find me. Although I do have a hot date with a tin of tuna tonight."

He smiled. I relaxed.

"Why do you want the job?"

"I don't want the job."

Silence.

Oliver leaned forward.

"As I see it, there are three lads in here who are up for this job: me, Tony, and Mike."

"That's right."

"I want you to give the job to Michael."

Oliver pointed out into the office in the direction of a small, timid-looking, middle-aged man.

As I looked around, I caught the cold stares of a handful of men who all looked totally unequipped to work in an office environment. The only person not staring back was Mike.

Oliver stood up, shook my hand again, and walked out of the cupboard door.

"Welcome to North Shore, Sir."

"Please, call me Euan."

"Thank you, Sir."

Tony was a no-show. Six foot four inches tall and built of solid muscle, Tony would later tell me that he had an urgent appointment at the medical centre for his crippling anxiety.

As the last man standing, Mike got the job.

Welcome to HMP North Shore

HMP North Shore was a Category A prison on the east coast of England.

Built on the site of a former RAF camp, the prison was twelve miles south of the old fishing port of Cragsholme and about a hundred miles away from anywhere anyone in their right mind would rather be.

As beachfront properties go, it offered little opportunity to view the wide expanse of sand on its doorstep. Not that the prison's male residents could ever hope to catch a glimpse of anything beyond the jail's 18-foot-high walls. The only life on the muddy flats below was a transient colony of grey seals dodging low-flying RAF jets on a still very active live bombing range.

On a good day, North Shore was home to 250 offenders. However, good days were hard to come by in a place like this. That number was often closer to 320.

With many of its population serving life terms, inmates could reasonably expect to share a pad with someone banged up for murder. Not that there were any angels in residence. Most of the men behind North Shore's walls had arrived here via a violent route.

I found myself in North Shore for very different reasons. Unlike most of the men behind these walls, I would be walking in and out of the front door every day. Despite this, I was still on the run.

I was on the run from my life as a freelance journalist, scraping together a living from all-too-irregular commissions and shifts in various London newsrooms. I was on the run from a flat I couldn't afford and the misery of early morning and late-night commutes between zones one and five. I was on the run from the mediocrity of a career I had dreamed of pursuing since I was ten years old. Be careful what you wish for.

I had landed a twelve-month stretch at North Shore covering maternity leave as the news editor of *The Hard Times*, a newspaper written for offenders by offenders. I'd been offered the job on the back of a feature I had somehow managed to squeeze into *The Guardian*. My story about the role of employment in the rehabilitation of offenders struck a chord with Bev, the paper's publisher. Following a hastily organised interview, where she tore the article apart (was it a slow news day?), she offered me the job on the spot, and I found myself on a train heading north.

Newsroom Scum

The Hard Times would be much like any other newsroom I'd ever worked in. The staff might have been locked in for the duration of their shifts, and the only bars these hacks were concerned with were on the windows, but to the untrained eye, our bustling office could have been the home of any small-town newspaper.

The weekly title was put together by a core team of around twelve offenders. They sat hunched over computers, writing and editing copy, working the phones, chasing quotes, sourcing images, and designing pages.

A small group of freelance contributors supported the in-house editorial team. These stringers came from across the English prison estate and were joined by a handful of ex-offenders on the outside. We even had a couple of celebrity columnists and letter writers, although the rules imposed by the offenders themselves—governed by a strict prison social hierarchy—prevented a few well-known fallen stars from securing any bylines in *The Hard Times*.

"He might have been the leader out there in his fucking Bacofoil suit, but the fucking nonce ain't getting his name in my newspaper."

Despite our unique situation, there was a lot of freedom given to everyone on the newspaper's staff. The office had unfettered access to the internet, email, and a landline telephone system. This didn't mean the team was trusted 100%. Every keystroke and phone call was recorded, and any unusual activity was flagged immediately to the Governor, who was both highly supportive and equally suspicious of the operation. Not that the newspaper had ever given the Governor any real cause for concern. That said, one of the many benefits of employing genuinely dishonest people was that there was nothing we couldn't cover up or hide.

The Governor certainly liked the positive PR the newspaper spun for his "progressive" prison regime. *The Hard Times* created more positive column inches regarding prison reform and offender rehabilitation in the mainstream press than any other programme.

The office worked on a one-strike-and-you're-out system. Any bad behaviour, and you'd be back to a mind-numbing job making breeze blocks or mopping floors.

Most of the guys working on *The Hard Times* knew they were onto a good thing and behaved accordingly.

But there was also a sense of pride on the team. On the outside, they might have been drug dealers, bank robbers, murderers, and general scum. But on the inside, and despite earning little more than £10 per week, many considered themselves serious journalists.

Professional scum.

Sally's Rule

I was joined in the newsroom by another civilian. Sally was an ex-prison officer who held the keys to the office.

While I was technically the boss, the day-to-day running of the operation rested on Sally's shoulders. She controlled the movement of the lads between the newsroom and the rest of the prison and managed any official prison business. But she also had an unofficial pastoral role. I believe she genuinely cared more about the men on our team than anyone had ever done before. The fact is, if they had known someone like Sally on the outside, most of them would not have found themselves on the inside.

I soon learned that there was an unwritten rule at *The Hard Times*: if you created a problem for Sally, you created a problem for yourself. Throughout her career, she had encountered some of the hardest and most dangerous men in the prison system. Recognising her compassion, they had nothing but respect for her.

Like any other newsroom, there was plenty of banter, but Sally took no shit.

Any misbehaviour in the office would typically be resolved by Sally banging her hand on her desk and issuing a disapproving stare. She was never angry, just disappointed—and the guys hated to disappoint Sally.

Real Hard Times

Before I set foot in the newsroom, Sally insisted that I visit the wing where most of my colleagues would be doing their real hard time. She told me that this visit would go further in explaining their psyche than any prison psychologist ever could.

Popular culture paints a picture of life on the inside, but nothing truly prepares you for the reality. I'm still trying to process how I felt about that first experience. One thing, however, was immediately obvious—this wasn't the holiday camp my former colleagues at the *Daily Mail* would have you believe was on offer at the taxpayer's expense. North Shore wasn't Center Parcs. It wasn't even a Travelodge. It was about as welcoming as a decommissioned oil rig.

The wing reminded me—both visually and in its underlying stench—of an old school gymnasium, a cavernous hall where every noise was amplified and echoed at migraine-inducing volume. Its four walls were lined with metal doors across two landings, each leading to a room no bigger than a council house bathroom. The central recreational area, about the size of a basketball court, had a rubberised blue floor, worn and dirty.

There was no comfort or fun to be found in this communal space. A pool table sat unused, missing its cues and balls. A broken TV bracket hung from one of the walls above a few mismatched tables and chairs.

"There was a bit of a riot here last week."

"Really?"

"Yeah. They think they'll get new stuff if they smash everything up."

Sally shook her head. "It really doesn't work like that."

As I took in the scene, my initial sense of foreboding was quickly replaced by a wave of depression. It was immediately clear: stress, boredom, isolation, and fear were the defining features of this place. Most of the time, absolutely nothing happened here. But when something did happen, it happened fast, and people got hurt.

At that moment, the wing was eerily quiet. There were only three other people besides Sally and me: a single female officer sat in her office, and two prisoners stood watching the fresh meat that had just arrived.

"Where is everyone?"

"Oh, they'll either be at work or in education."

"What about those guys?"

"That's Paedo Steve and Harley. They're working."

A doughy man leaned on a mop, watching our every move, his fat, spittle-covered tongue poking out from his toothless mouth.

"He's a paedophile?"

"Actually, no. He wouldn't last five minutes in here if he was a beast. The lads on the wing just think he looks like one, and the nickname stuck."

"Poor bugger.'

"Yeah. Someday, someone's going to take it seriously—no smoke without fire—and kill the stupid sod. The lads can be cruel, but he's as thick as shit, and I think he likes the attention when they start shouting 'paedo' at him."

In the corner, a younger blur of a man stood polishing the handset of one of the wing's pay phones with nervous energy.

"So everyone who's not on remand has to either have a job or be in education. But there's not enough work to go around, and those two don't have an academic brain cell between them. So he mops this side of the wing, and his mate over there cleans the phones."

"Whether they need it or not."

"Well, he's certainly got a strong work ethic. He polishes those phones eight hours a day. Never stands still. There's usually another guy who mops the other side, but I guess he's visiting the medical centre this morning."

"Sick?"

"Sick of mopping floors."

"Yeah, I get that."

"To be honest, they love a trip to the nurse. You'll never meet a bigger bunch of hypochondriacs than in prison. You'll see that when you get into the office."

"Really?"

"I literally spend half my life walking perfectly healthy lads from the office to the medical centre and back again."

"Breaks up their routine, I suppose. Must be mind-numbing."

"They're all a little bit mental, really. But aren't we all? Some, like Steve over there, really shouldn't be in here. He's institutionalised, can't function anywhere else. But that's North Shore. It's not that bad, really. You should see Hull."

"The prison or the city?"

"Both."

Sally led me towards an open cell door. "Hey, Harley, do you mind if Euan here has a look at your pad?"

The phone polisher dropped the handset and rushed over, bristling with nervous energy.

"Sure, check it out. This is my pad."

The three of us filed in and wholly occupied the tiny room. A set of children's bunk beds dominated the cell, the cheap, rusty frames looking barely strong enough to hold a child, let alone a grown man.

"So, there's two of you in here?"

Harley nodded. "This is mine and Dominic's pad. Dominic killed a man. He ate his fucking face. Hope he doesn't eat me."

"Now, Harley. I don't think that's true, is it?"

"No, Miss."

Harley's posture changed. It was like his battery had suddenly gone flat.

"Not much space for two blokes in here. Must be difficult."

Silence.

"According to some European human rights law, each of these cells should house one man. But we get overcrowded, so a lot of the lads have to share. Isn't that right, Harley?"

Harley nodded.

"David Cameron's lot prefers to pay fines to the EU instead of building more prisons. They want to lock more people up, but there's no space."

Harley's eyes lit up. "Fucking Cameron. He's a muppet. Right, Miss?"

Sally smiled.

The only other furniture was a desk and a single plastic chair. A *Katie Price* autobiography sat on the table. Sally picked it up.

"We've got a half-decent library service. Offenders can request any book deposited with the British Library." She carefully placed the book back down. "That's Dominic's."

Harley pulled a serious face. "I like *Katie Price*. But I prefer her earlier work."

He glanced up at his collection of soft porn taped to the ceiling above his bunk

I tried not to notice the stainless steel toilet bowl barely hidden behind a shower curtain.

"How long do you spend in here?"

"They took our TVs off us last week. Even though I stayed in my pad when it all kicked off, they still took mine. Still got my PlayStation, but you can't play *FIFA* without a TV. Stupid. Put that in your stupid paper."

"Come on, Harley."

"Sorry, Miss."

Sally sighed. "They spend far too much time locked up. If the prison's short on staff—and it always is—they can be banged up for 22 hours a day at weekends."

The room fell silent. I couldn't imagine sharing this space, let alone with a violent roommate and a stinking toilet.

"That's why they love coming to work. And why they actually work hard."

In that moment, it all made perfect sense.

The Road to Hard Times

My days at *The Hard Times* started early. I don't drive. I never really needed a car in London and never thought I'd find myself working in such a remote location. As such, I arrived at the prison gates at 7:30 each morning courtesy of a local taxi firm, Gabe's Cabs. The name made it sound grander than it was. There was only one cab—a blue Nissan Sunny—and one driver, Gabe.

Gabe was a friendly chap, maybe ten years my senior. At first, I didn't think we had much in common. I assumed he saw me as a soft southerner, probably a little too woke for his liking. There wasn't a bad bone in his body, but he had his prejudices—views shaped by a life that hadn't quite panned out the way he'd hoped. That said, we quickly bonded over a shared love of music. Gabe spoke with authority and at length on subjects like The Beatles' early years, why Oasis could never match Lennon and McCartney's output, and how Johnny Cash, not Elvis, invented rock and roll.

Gabe *loved* Johnny Cash. Like Cash, he was fascinated by prisons and their inmates. Unlike Cash, his interest was more voyeuristic than compassionate.

The guys behind HMP North Shore's walls both fascinated and disgusted him in equal measure. If I ever mentioned someone by name, he'd immediately ask what they'd done and how long their sentence was. Always disappointed by my lack of detail, he'd scour the internet for news articles about their crimes, arrests, and trials to fuel our conversations.

"Fucking scum. I don't know how you can work with them."

To be fair, Gabe had an unusual set of morals himself.

"Went to see that *Blues Brothers* show at Cragsholme Auditorium last night. Bloody brilliant."

"Yeah? Good show?"

"Yeah. Really good. The band were tight—more of a rock show than a musical, really. You know, nothing queer about the *Blues Brothers*."

"Sure."

Gabe viewed homosexuals much like he viewed criminals—entertaining, but best kept at arm's length.

"It really was great. But there was something I didn't like."

"Oh? What was that?"

"The backing singers."

"The backing singers?"

"Yeah. Beautiful girls. You know, black, but I mean *really* good looking ones. One of them had really big, you know…"

He took his hands off the steering wheel to demonstrate the size of the backing singer's breasts.

"Go on?"

"Well, you know me. I'm no prude, but their dresses were too fucking short."

"Too short?"

"Yeah. I mean, you could almost see what they had for dinner."

"What was that then?"

"Ha! Ham fucking sandwiches. You know what I mean, though. Don't you?"

"So you don't like pretty girls in short dresses flashing their knickers. Are you going queer on me, Gabe?"

I was throwing his outdated insults back at him playfully.

"No mate, I'm bloody not!"

"OK! So what's your problem?"

"Well, there's a time and a place, isn't there?"

"Is there?"

"It's the wife, see."

"Go on?"

"She sees me looking at them birds with their bloody long legs and their big tits for a second, and the night is fucking ruined."

"Ah! Got it. She knows you too well."

"Bloody tarts!"

He was getting quite agitated.

"Watch your blood pressure, Gabe."

"Fuck off."

He took his eyes off the road for a little longer than I was comfortable with.

"You're beginning to sound like the wife now. You know, the other day I caught her checking the car for KFC wrappers. Always telling me they're not good for my blood pressure. I'll tell you what's not good for my blood pressure."

"Black girls in short dresses?"

Gabe also had a problem with the tax man.

"Haven't paid it in years. My accountant keeps telling me how much I owe, and I keep telling him it's too much. I'd rather spend the money on my caravan. They can take it out of my house—whatever's left of it—when I'm dead."

"Bloody hell, Gabe! You'll end up in jail, working for me on the paper if you're not careful."

"I could do with the holiday."

"Well, your wife will have no problem with you and those leggy birds in there."

"That'll keep her happy."

As he dropped me off at the prison gates, Gabe would shout the same joke from his taxi window, laughing at his own comedic genius as he sped off each day.

"Don't drop the soap, mate. Just don't drop the fucking soap!"

A Dog Named Barry

A large black sign in reverse block text greeted all visitors to the prison with a list of items they were prohibited from taking inside. Alongside the obvious—drugs, tobacco, cash, firearms, and explosives—were a few items that would generally be quite problematic for a journalist not to carry. Mobile phones, computers, cameras, and recording equipment all carried the threat of a ten-year jail sentence if smuggled in.

The Hard Times had negotiated some concessions. I did have permission to carry a laptop on the understanding that it didn't have a webcam. This was, in itself, a problem. Where the hell do you buy a laptop without a webcam? It's such an unusual specification request that they actually sell at a premium. Less is more.

Permission to carry mobile phones, cameras, and recording equipment was entirely out of the question. Even the cheapest mobile phone is worth thousands of pounds behind bars, and just carrying one into the prison would put us at risk of violence. As for recording equipment and cameras, we'd have to go "old school" with a pen and a pad, sourcing any images we needed from outside the prison.

Considering North Shore's status as a Category A prison, it was surprising how lax their security was. In the twelve months I worked there, I was never once searched, asked to walk through the airport-style metal detectors, or had my bags scanned upon entering.

If they had ever taken the opportunity to pat me down, they would have found all manner of concealed goods—nothing illegal. Maybe just a stash of mini pork pies, a box of Mr Kipling cakes, or a few bags of Haribo. These were essential productivity tools at *The Hard Times*. Unable to offer any cash bonuses and knowing how lousy prison food was, I soon learned that an illicit savoury snack or sweet treat acted as an incredible incentive to get the newspaper out on time.

In lieu of any serious security checks, I'd flash my passport at the officer at the front desk, lock my mobile phone and wallet in a small locker, and proceed to walk through the prison's airlock system.

The airlock worked on the principle that its two timed electronic doors, operated by an officer at the front desk, could never be opened simultaneously. On entering the airlock, there was a considerable delay between the first door closing and the next opening, which could not be overridden. Even if a determined escapee managed to get off the wing, through the numerous gates in the yard, and into the reception area, they would quickly find themselves trapped in the airlock.

After passing through the airlock, there was a second reception area where I would wait for Sally or an available officer to escort me to the office. Occasionally, I'd be met by an officer with a very excitable sniffer dog.

"Don't worry. Barry's very friendly. You'll only have a problem if he suddenly sits down."

"Your dog is called Barry?"

"Yeah, the missus is a big fan of Manilow."

"Ha! Had to be a reason why he developed a taste for drugs."

Thankfully, Barry didn't have a Haribo habit.

The reception was furnished with a couple of heavy-duty, uncomfortable-looking sofas and a coffee table where you might find an old copy of *The Hard Times* and some trade union magazines. But it was the notice board that was essential reading.

There were posters for various social activities for officers and their families, details regarding support groups for alcohol, drug, and mental health issues, and updates on prisoner numbers and movements. While I was reassured by a notice stating that HMP North Shore had a zero-tolerance policy towards bullying and violence, I was never quite sure if this was aimed at the officers or the offenders.

But it was the updates regarding contraband thrown over the prison walls that I found especially entertaining. Most days, this would include small amounts of drugs, SIM cards, and burner mobile phones. But occasionally, more substantial packages made their way over the wire—cartons of cigarettes, weapons, significant bundles of money, and, once, even a still-warm supermarket rotisserie chicken.

These well-timed deliveries would put your average Amazon driver to shame. Prior to a package landing in the yard, a fight would be staged to distract any officers, allowing a courier to conceal the package and smuggle it onto the wing. I don't know what percentage of packages made it to their intended recipients, but the volume of goods seized suggested this was a numbers game.

Entirely why the police didn't stop anyone with a good throwing arm who just so happened to be randomly walking their dog around the prison wall in such a remote location was beyond me. Like many things in this place, I suspect it was a bit of a game—one where both sides were allowed to win from time to time.

The Key

Sally would meet me at reception most mornings.

Despite being a civilian, she wore a prison keychain, belt, and pouch.

"We'll get you a set of these soon. Save me coming to get you. You just need to fill out some forms, and then we'll get you on a course."

"Are you serious? That can't be right."

"Sure. Why not?"

"I mean, I'm just a bloke off the street. They really shouldn't be giving a key to the jailhouse to any old Tom, Dick, or Harry that comes along. What could possibly go wrong with that stupid idea?"

"Ha! Plenty. But it'll save me coming to get you every morning. I get enough steps in walking the dog and escorting the lads to their various appointments. I don't need to be running backwards and forwards after you."

It's a myth that prison officers carry big bunches of keys. Every officer at HMP North Shore had just one key—for every gate, door, and cell.

"When you've locked or unlocked a door, you put the key straight back in the pouch. If it's in your hand for any length of time, you keep it shielded from sight. These buggers are crafty. They just need a good look at the key, and they'll have one made up in no time."

"Really?"

"Yeah, it happened a couple of years back."

"Someone escaped?"

"No. No one has ever escaped from here. When they built the place, apparently, they hired some ex-SAS guys to test the system. They didn't even get off the wing."

"So what happened with the key?"

"They carved a decent copy out of a piece of wood. Got them off the wing and into the yard before it fell apart. But it just shows you."

"So what happened then?"

"They had to change every lock in the prison. Can you imagine how much that cost?"

"Wow. I can imagine. Thousands."

"Tens of thousands. If a key gets lost, all hell breaks loose. And you don't want to know what happens if you ever take your key home by mistake."

"What happens then?"

"Ha! Well, your predecessor found out the hard way."

"Go on."

"First thing she knew about it, her front door had been kicked off its hinges, and a load of armed coppers were screaming at her to get out of bed. Her boyfriend literally shat himself."

Being a keyholder seemed a responsibility far beyond my pay grade. I never did fill out that form and found multiple excuses not to go on the course.

We walked from the reception area onto the central yard. Small groups of offenders congregated at various gates, chatting to mates and shouting across the central area to the residents of other wings, waiting for the working day to begin.

Everyone was always happy to see Sally.

"Morning, Miss. How are you today?"

Sally stopped to speak with a man on the other side of the wire.

"I'm good, Brian. Thank you. How's that beautiful daughter of yours? I saw her coming in to visit you the other day."

"She's good, thanks for asking, Miss. She just got into college."

"She's a smart girl."

"Must get it from her mother, Miss. Certainly didn't get it from me."

"Don't put yourself down, Brian. You're doing well on that Open University course, aren't you?"

"I'm enjoying it, Miss. Who'd have thought when I came in here, eh?"

Sally turned to me as we walked away.

"You wouldn't believe how smart some of the lads are here. A lot of them have got incredible potential but no direction, so they make stupid decisions."

"What decisions did he make?"

"Who? Brian? Well, like most of the people in here, he just failed to engage his brain."

"Go on?"

"Complete accident, apparently. And funnily enough, that was Brian's line of defence. Someone spilled a drink down his wife's front, and he killed the poor sod with a single punch. He didn't mean to do it. Half of them never do. But it landed him in here with the other half, who, let's just say, were perhaps more motivated to do whatever they did."

We carried on walking.

"The thing is, we all know someone like Brian. He's an instant arsehole—just add alcohol. You know what I mean."

"Sure."

"You blokes are all the same with a few pints in you. Brian was just unlucky."

"Not as unlucky as the guy he hit."

"Yep. But what can you do? He made a mistake, and he's got to pay for it. On one hand, it's too much for a guy like Brian to end up in a place like this for eight years. On the other hand, he killed a guy, and that's a debt he can never pay back."

"It's difficult."

"It's cruel, no matter how you look at it. Nobody wins. My best advice is, try not to get emotionally attached to anyone in this place. It'll drive you insane."

"Are you speaking from personal experience?"

"Do I look fucking crazy?"

She winked at me and playfully punched my upper arm.

"Don't answer that."

News Radar

It would be an understatement to describe my first few days at HMP North Shore as an assault on my senses. I was bombarded with new sights, sounds, and emotions—so much so that it took a while for my hyperactive mind to settle enough for me to fully focus on putting a newspaper together. But that didn't mean story ideas weren't already presenting themselves.

I've always believed that a good journalist lives and dies by the strength of their story ideas. As a freelancer, I considered the day wasted if I didn't make at least one pitch. My news radar was always set to high alert.

I didn't have to wait long for my first lead at North Shore.

Gabe pitched it to me on my very first day, as we drove out of the staff car park.

A small orange tent had been pitched on the grass verge, just a couple of feet outside the prison's perimeter.

Next to the tent, a man with a deep tan and a footlong beard sat in a camping chair, cooking his dinner on a small gas stove.

"Who's that guy?"

"He's been here for years. Bit of a local celebrity. They call him Jimmy."

"What's his story?"

"He's an ex-con, apparently. Got released and barely made it off the premises. Must like it here. You should write about him."

I made a mental note to follow up on that idea as soon as possible.

The Model Employee

Mike took his job as my assistant very seriously. Every morning, without fail, he greeted me with the same words.

"M-m-morning, Sir. How are you today? B-b-black c-coffee?"

At times, I felt that Mike showed me too much respect. He would never turn his back on me, always taking two steps backward before rushing off to make my coffee—then returning with one of the cakes I had smuggled in for the team, carefully placed on a plastic plate.

"No thanks, Mike. They're for the lads."

"B-b-but you are o-one of the lads, Sir."

Mike had the look of a beaten man, as if he were battling permanent exhaustion and shame. I liked Mike. But, if I'm honest, I also felt sorry for him.

Despite his timid nature, Mike was surprisingly well-respected by the other prisoners. No one overly mocked his stammer or his slight build. In a place where any sign of weakness was usually an open invitation for attack, Mike was somehow immune. I assumed it was because he was simply a nice guy—until I reminded myself that this wasn't a place for nice guys.

Mike was brilliant at his job. He primarily worked as an editorial assistant, typing up handwritten copy from our outside contributors. But where he really excelled was proofreading. He was nothing short of forensic in his search for typos and misplaced commas.

He worked hard, never complained when the workload piled up, and the only time he stepped away from his desk was to make me a coffee—a model employee.

I couldn't imagine what Mike had done to end up in a place like this. Had he fallen on hard times, stolen from the office petty cash, and somehow wound up in a Category A prison due to some ridiculous clerical error?

Still, I stuck to my rule of only discussing my colleagues' crimes if they brought them up first. It was none of my business, and I didn't want to find myself judging them and suddenly not liking them. God knows, some of them had done terrible things.

Ignorance was bliss. As long as they met their deadlines and got the paper to print on time, they were all as good as gold to me.

Hard Labour

I'd soon learn that the work ethic of my little team was nothing short of impressive. While there was plenty of banter, the lads worked harder than most of the journalists I'd had the pleasure of working with on the outside. They were undoubtedly less burdened with hangovers.

Harry, our letters editor and the oldest member of the team, had a theory that hard work was hardwired into many of the people who ended up at North Shore.

"It's not easy being a crook. In fact, it takes a lot of hard work."

"Really?"

"Yeah. You look at most of the young lads in here, and they're in because of the old…"

Harry pulled up his shirt sleeve and frantically started tapping his inner arm, mimicking the act of raising a vein.

"Drugs?"

"Yeah. I mean, being a junkie is a real commitment. It takes a lot of effort to stay medicated. That stuff's not cheap."

"I guess."

"And then, on the other side of the fence—you know, selling the shit—well, there's plenty of people in here who can tell you all about that. Fucking hard work. Not that I would have anything to do with that crap."

Harry considered himself an old-school villain—a good old-fashioned bank robber.

"Do you know how much work goes into planning a bank job? You've got to be sure there's enough cash in the bank to make it worth the risk. You've got to get away and stash the cash somewhere safe. And then you've got to know how to clean it. You can't just spend it."

"Doesn't always work out though, does it? I mean, this isn't your first time in a place like this, is it?"

"Well, it's a bit of an occupational hazard when you're in my line of work. It's a numbers game, really. Do a few jobs, get lifted for one. A few years here and there. It all works out in the end. I was looking forward to retiring down to Portugal in a few years."

Harry's dreams of the Algarve were washed away when he was handed a life sentence for his last job.

"Sixteen years I've been here now. Should have been five or six at most."

"So what happened?"

"My mate decided it would be a good idea to put some bloody bullets in his gun. Normally, you just wave an empty pistol in someone's face, and they shit themselves. Just ask Alex over there—he did his one with a kid's toy."

Alex looked up and shook his head but said nothing.

"Bloody idiot shot the security guard, didn't he? I'm a bank robber, not a murderer. I was sent down for joint enterprise. It's not right."

With perfect timing, the office radio started playing *Bankrobber* by The Clash.

"Harry, they're playing your song. You never hurt nobody."

Before you knew it, the entire office was singing along.

"Fuck off! You're all bastards, the lot of you."

Harry was clearly feigning outrage. He lowered his voice.

"They're all good lads, really. A bit of banter is good for morale. Hey, talking of low morale, I saw the worst thing I've ever seen in my sixteen years in this place last night."

"What was that?"

"Went over to Mike's pad before lock-up yesterday to borrow a book he was on about. He was sat there taking a shit. Door wide open. Didn't even pull the curtain around him. Fucking bunch of animals in here."

Perhaps sensing he was being talked about, Mike looked up with a cheeky smile.

"You're a fucking animal, ain't ya, Mike?"

Mike howled like a wolf.

"W-w-what can I say, Harry? I'm f-f-fucking in-institutionalised."

"You fucking stink, you daft cunt."

"C-c-c-coffee, Sir?"

Survival of the Fittest

Most of the *Hard Times* crew had been in the system for years. Many had spent their time sticking it to the man before finally coming to the conclusion that it might be better to play by a different set of rules. To this end, they took part in rehabilitation programmes and special courses to address their personal challenges.

Gary, one of our news writers, was an apparent model prisoner. He volunteered as a mentor on the prison's induction wing—a place most inmates wouldn't relish spending any more time than they had to. But Gary chose to live there full-time, hoping to help young prisoners transition more smoothly into the general population.

"I used to work on the door at a club in Huddersfield. I'm used to the odd ruck. But I've never seen anything like that wing."

"Is it rough?"

"It's fucking Bedlam."

"Really?"

"Yeah, so many lads arrive on that wing ready for a fight. In reality, they're all fucking cowards. They go in looking for weak targets and try to get the first punch in—create some sort of reputation as someone you don't want to mess with."

"Understandable."

"It's dog eat dog, mate. Honestly, we consider it a quiet week if nobody gets stabbed. And you wouldn't believe how many kids can't take it and are found swinging in their pads in their first couple of days here. It's survival of the fittest. Proper *Lord of the Flies* shit."

According to Gary, drugs were the biggest problem on the wing. He knew a thing or two about drugs and the problems they caused—he wouldn't have been in North Shore if it weren't for his purely commercial interest in substances.

"There are either too many drugs or not enough. People come in rattling like fuck. Do anything for a fix. So they start building up debts they can never pay off. People take advantage of that."

"So how do you stop it?"

"Well, you can't. But I can offer some quiet words of advice. Plus, look at me—I'm fucking stacked. Most of the kids that come in here are so malnourished and full of junk. They see me and don't want to mess. And if they do, well, let's just say I don't always play by the rules."

"And the prison officers?"

"They see what they want to see."

"So what do you get out of it?"

"A lot of brownie points for my parole hearing in a couple of years. Oh, and a single pad."

"You don't have to share?"

"No, man. I fucking love it. I've got my radio, I've got my books, and I've got time to, well, you know."

"Peace and quiet?"

"In this place? Not a fucking chance. There's always some cunt kicking off or an alarm bell ringing. No, I've just got my own space. As long as that door is locked, I don't have to deal with anyone else's shit."

Gary taught me a lot about prison politics.

"Listen, we get on alright in here, don't we?"

"Sure."

"You're a nice bloke. You treat everyone in the office with respect."

"I try."

"The lads like that. You're not a con, and you're not a screw, so the dynamic is kind of unique. But know this—if you were on that wing and you had something I wanted, I'd take it from you."

"Really?"

"Nice trainers you've got on there, Sir. What size are you? Ten?"

"Nine."

"Oh, you'll be alright this time. You can keep 'em."

Therapy

While some prisoners were clearly more complex than others, Tony was an open book. He'd spent most of his adult life under the care of a prison psychologist who encouraged him to talk through his problems. And boy, could he talk.

"I'm clocking off early today, Sir."

"Please, call me Euan. Why? What's up?"

"I've got an appointment with the shrink. It's my nerves, you see."

Tony never really struck me as an anxious person. Even in his quiet moments, he bounced around the office like a hyperactive toddler.

"It's this place. You lose hope when you're in for a long stretch like me."

"How long are you doing?"

"Eighteen years. There's cunts in here that got less for murder. Do you know what I did?"

"No. And I don't—"

"Just robbery. They made up the bit about extreme violence. Only tied the bugger up and gave him a little slap. Didn't really hurt him I think he was after some compo. Fucking bent bastard. Everyone's on the make these days, aren't they?"

In all fairness, I'd witnessed Tony's penchant for violence in the office many times before. At least once a week, without warning, he'd select a random victim, wrestle them to the ground, and pin their arms to their sides with his legs—before planting a massive kiss on their forehead to rapturous applause from the rest of the guys.

"So, why did you get so long?"

"Well, turns out there was a lot of cash in that security van we stopped, and they never recovered it. Bastards think I'm loaded, but I never saw a penny of it. Even if I did know where that money went, they'll be watching me like a hawk the moment I get out of here. That money's long gone."

I got on well with Tony. I wouldn't say we were friends, but I enjoyed our conversations. I quickly learned that those conversations weren't exactly private. There was one person particularly interested in them.

His name was Robert Tinker, and he was literally bad news.

Tinker

Tinker was a tabloid hack with a reputation for going further than most to get a story.

His photo was prominently displayed in the prison reception area, accompanied by a note stating that he was banned from entering every establishment in the UK prison estate. Not that it stopped him from phoning me weekly.

Speaking to him reminded me of the *Spitting Image* caricatures of journalists on TV in the eighties—pigs at the feeding trough, wearing fedoras with press passes tucked into the brim.

"You know I used to work there, don't you?"

"Yeah. You were an officer?"

"Kind of."

At the time, Tinker had an interest in one of North Shore's more high-profile guests.

"Donald Nairn. Horrible nonce. My readers wanted to see that he was getting his just deserts."

As an undercover journalist, Tinker had applied for a job as a prison officer, gone through basic training, and found himself walking the wings of North Shore.

According to him, Nairn spent most of his time in solitary and on suicide watch. The door to his cell was left open 24 hours a day, with an officer permanently stationed outside.

"Nobody wanted to do it. I volunteered. He couldn't even take a shit or knock one out without me watching. I don't even want to say I smuggled a camera in. It was in my lunchbox. The idiots on the gate don't check for anything. Most of them are still pissed from the night before."

The photo Tinker took of Nairn relaxing in his cell made the front pages. It also made him a lot of money and stirred up plenty of shit in the prison system.

Tinker was arrested for lying on his application forms and smuggling a camera into the prison, but eventually, all charges were dropped.

"Too fucking embarrassing for the establishment. It literally said on my passport when I applied for the job that I was a journalist. I had a huge byline on the front page of the *News of the World* the day before they offered me the job. My name was everywhere. Robert fucking big balls Tinker."

Nairn killed himself a few days after the photos were published. Apparently, the officer who replaced Tinker on suicide watch wasn't so attentive.

"So, how can I help you? You got a story?"

"No. But you might."

I waited.

"Big Tony. My sources tell me he speaks to you. I want to know what he's done with the money."

"Mate. You *do* know these phone calls are recorded—right?"

"Yeah. But is anyone really listening?"

"Bye, Mr Tinker."

"You know where to find me if you hear anything. I can make it worth your while."

In reality, Tinker didn't need me as a source. The prison leaked stories to the press all the time, resulting in occasional staff purges and, once—much to the Governor's embarrassment—widespread media coverage and the rapid cancellation of the annual Christmas pantomime on the VP wing.

Smart Guys

Almost every story we ran in *The Hard Times* resonated with the guys in the newsroom in one way or another. Reports about prison closures leading to greater overcrowding, catering budget cuts reducing the quality of their food, or proposed smoking bans and gym charges all had a direct impact on their lives.

Passions could sometimes run high, and it was difficult to separate the story from personal experience to create a balanced piece. I often had to remind the team what their job was.

"In this newspaper, we have a news section and an editorial and features section. If you're writing news, I want facts. There's no room for your feelings in a news story. The only emotions should come from the quotes of the people you're interviewing. If you want to talk about your feelings, move over to the features desk or write a column."

The lads always pushed back.

"But this is fucked. They can't do this! I *need* to write about it."

"Listen. You know where anger gets you. Angry men aren't the most productive people, and when anger *does* fuel the creative process, it's never sustainable. I don't want you burning out on me."

Sometimes, they just needed to get something off their chests, and I was a good listener.

My desk was directly across from Harry's. Harry liked to talk.

"I like that you spend so much time with the lads. Makes them feel normal, you know? Like they've got a proper job."

"They *do* have a proper job."

"Yeah. But talking to you takes their minds off the fact they're stuck in here with old cunts like me."

"Yeah, poor buggers. Stuck in here with you. But you know what? That's exactly what I want. If they feel normal, if they actually enjoy coming in here, I'll get better work out of them. It's totally selfish of me, really."

I always let them steer the conversation. I didn't want to remind them too much of how restricted their lives were compared to mine—someone who could just walk out of the door at the end of a shift.

"Do you have a mobile phone?"

"Yeah. Of course. It's locked up at reception."

"One of those smartphones?"

"Yeah. It's an iPhone."

"You can take photos and shit with that, right?"

Knowing that a man had never seen a smartphone in real life highlighted just how long some of them had spent behind bars. It was a sobering thought.

"Sure. Photos, videos, it plays music, movies—there's an app for pretty much everything these days."

"I had a mobile when I worked on the markets in Birmingham. You couldn't do any of that shit with it, though. It was the size of a brick. A *big* brick. Thought I was a right Billy Bollocks walking around with it stuck to my ear. But I'll definitely get one of those smartphones when I get out."

Daniel, our website manager, joined the conversation and slowly moved towards my desk.

"Why would you want a smartphone, Harry?"

"What do you mean? Why *wouldn't* I want one? Got to keep up with the times, Danny boy."

"Listen. If you think about it, every cunt in here is *in* here because of their mobile phones."

"How so?"

"Well, do you think the fucking plod caught M-M-M-Mike over there in his orange Renault because of their forensic police skills?"

"F-f-f-fuck off."

Mike joined our little huddle.

"No. They just put a call into Vodafone or whoever and tracked his phone to his boyfriend's flat."

"H-h-he wasn't my b-b-boyfriend, you cheeky c-c-c c-c-c—"

"Cunt?"

"F."

"And Oliver over there? His phone led the police straight to the shed in his mate's mother's garden, where he was hiding out. Stupid bugger didn't think to turn it off and kept calling his girlfriend. The police didn't *catch* any of us. They just followed the phone signals. I'll stick to public payphones when I'm out and about."

"I thought you were a changed man? All rehabilitated with Jesus on your side?"

"I am. I just don't want any cunt knowing where I am. That's fucking creepy if you ask me."

"You might be right, Daniel. But there's another reason you don't want a smartphone."

"Oh yeah? What's that then, smartarse?"

"You're a cunt, and nobody likes you. Who would you call? Not your girlfriend."

BANG!

Sally's hands crashed down on her desk.

"Let's get back to work, gentlemen. You too, Euan. And Harry—stop causing trouble."

We all hesitated for a moment before shuffling back to our stations. But just as I settled back into my chair, Harry leaned forward and nodded in the direction of Daniel.

"He killed his girlfriend. And nobody knows what happened to the one before that. He's a creepy sod. Needs putting back in his box."

The Quiet Man

Alex, our picture editor, was a man of very few words. In fact, he was quite the moody sod. Despite this, everyone in the office had a positive opinion of him. Sally was a particular fan.

"That man shouldn't be in here. He's not like the other lads."

"Really? He robbed a bank, didn't he? I mean, that's not unlike quite a few other lads in here."

Sensing my scepticism, Sally argued in Alex's defence.

"There were some extenuating circumstances. And besides, he never hurt anyone. Bloody hell, he did it with a *toy* gun."

"But the young girl behind the counter didn't know that. She's probably still in therapy."

"Yeah, but he's not like anyone else in here, is he?"

Sally told me that Alex had once been a successful businessman before falling on hard times.

"He lost his business, was about to lose his house, his wife was long gone, and he started to think he might never see his kids again."

Alex might have been a high-flyer in a previous life, but he was certainly no criminal mastermind.

Within minutes of stealing a paltry £1,200 from his local branch of the Halifax, he attempted to deposit it into his personal savings account at Barclays—just across the street. He was still wearing his balaclava.

"Desperate times call for desperate measures. You don't know what you'd do in those circumstances, do you?"

I was fairly sure I wouldn't go running into a bank on my local high street with a water pistol.

I couldn't help but think that Alex actually had a lot in common with many of the men who found themselves in North Shore. Most of them were victims of circumstance. Alex had just fallen from a greater height.

He was the classic example of a prisoner who kept his head down, his nose clean, and just did his time.

It was hard to start a conversation with him. And believe me, I tried.

"Are you a metalhead?"

"No."

"It's just the long hair. I thought you might be into metal."

"No. Just not letting any cunt in here come at me with a pair of scissors."

"I saw a few big bands back in the day. Iron Maiden, Megadeth, Anthrax—you know, at the Hammersmith Odeon. It was still the Odeon back then."

No answer.

I was waffling. Not that he seemed to notice. He was completely fixated on a blurred green shape on his screen. After a long moment, he finally turned to me.

"Can you tell that's a crocodile?"

"Not really, Alex. What story is this for?"

"Ex-con. Got a job in a fucking zoo."

"Well, I guess he knows all about life behind bars."

It was a poor joke and deserved zero response.

The only time I ever heard Alex become animated was after lunch.

"Seriously. Do you call that food?"

"Was it that bad?"

"Have you ever seen a fat man in here?"

To describe Alex as *lean* would be an understatement.

It was true—Alex didn't really fit in here. He never tried to. Maybe he didn't *want* to fit in. Or maybe he really *was* different from everyone else on the team.

Right and Wrong

Oliver most definitely *fitted in*. If *The Hard Times* had an unofficial leader, he was probably it. Alpha male all the way.

Oliver might have killed two men, but he was no criminal. Not in his mind, nor in anyone else's in here. In many ways, he was a hero.

He was a prime example of how circumstances could land you in big trouble.

Before he wound up in this place, he told me he'd always been a good lad who knew the difference between right and wrong—despite a hard start in life that saw him and his younger sister growing up in care.

"I'd been out of the kids' home for about two years when I heard what those two bastards had done to Katie."

"What happened?"

Oliver shook his head. This wasn't something he was ready to talk about.

"I was all she had, and I let her down. But I sorted it out, and the rest is history. You should know this, though—I give zero fucks that those two cunts are in the ground. I'd do it again in a heartbeat."

"And Katie? Is she okay?"

"Well, it took her some time to get over what I did. She hated me at first. Thought those guys were her friends. But now we're a bit older, and she's got kids, I think we're getting there. Yeah, we're in a better place now."

The Myth of Rehabilitation

The concept of rehabilitation was a much-discussed topic in the office and in the pages of *The Hard Times*.

Some of the team truly believed the paper was their chance to turn their lives around. Others were more sceptical.

Oliver, despite his commitment to the project, was not a great believer in the process.

"You know a lot of us are just playing a game in here, don't you?"

"What game?"

"We do and say the right things at the right time. Work our way through various programmes, tick a few boxes, kiss enough backsides, and even people like me can live in hope of seeing the outside world again."

"So, in your case, life doesn't mean life?"

"Oh, life means life. But that sentence doesn't have to be served in a place like this. When I get out, I'll be on licence for the rest of my life. If I so much as drop a piece of litter in the street or park on a double yellow, I'll be back here quicker than Mike can say, 'It it it w-w-wasn't m-m-m-me.'"

Without raising his head from his work, Mike threw a well-aimed pencil at Oliver, missing by a fraction of an inch.

"C-c-c-cheeky c-cunt."

Both men laughed.

"So you think you'll get out?"

"I've got a five-year plan. Might take a bit longer, but I really hope to be out before my 40th birthday."

It struck me for the first time that we were similar in age. Oliver seemed much younger.

"You got sent down at 19?"

"Yeah. Been here man and boy."

"Ever been in trouble before then?"

"No. Not really."

"You must have been scared coming in here for the first time."

"Yeah, I was. But then I bumped into some of the kids I grew up with in the care home, and it was alright after that."

"So what will you do on the outside? Be a journalist?"

"Nah. That's not on the cards."

"But you're good at it. I'd give you a reference."

"That's not the way it works."

"How so?"

"Listen, if you buy into that rehabilitation shit, you're stupider than you look. No offence, sir."

"None taken."

"But you're doing a great job here."

"Maybe. It gives me something to focus on while I'm in here. And I do enjoy it. But they won't let me do this on the outside. They don't want you to work when you're out on licence."

"How so?"

"They like to keep an eye on you. Move you into a hostel—a halfway house, if you like. Don't really like you moving about. It's much easier if you stay put and don't go to work."

"Wow. That sounds depressing."

"Yeah. But I've got plans."

"Go on."

"Need to get my hands on some of Tony's money."

Tony reacted suddenly, leaping over his desk.

"THERE'S NO FUCKING MONEY, MATE!"

Mike ran between them.

"C-c-calm down, Tony. H-h-he's joking."

"HOW MANY FUCKING TIMES? THERE'S NO FUCKING MONEY!"

Then suddenly—BANG! It was like someone had thrown a hand grenade into the office.

All eyes turned to Sally.

It was hard not to be impressed by her control of the situation. She was like a lion tamer. These men could have torn her apart, but they obeyed every word she said.

Price of the Game

The lads handled regret in different ways. For some, their only regret was being caught.

"Was it worth it, Gary?"

"What do you mean?"

"Well, I mean, did it seem like a good idea at the time? You know, all the stuff you did that got you sent here."

I had broken my first rule for survival in this place—I was sticking my nose into something that might just get it broken.

"Well, in hindsight, no. But at the time—fuck yeah."

"Go on."

"We had it all. Nice cars. Money in the bank. Women throwing themselves at us. I walked around that town like I was Ronnie fucking Kray. People looked up to us. They really did. But they were also scared shitless of us. That felt great."

"So you were living the dream."

"Yeah, but it quickly became a nightmare."

"So when did it go wrong?"

"Well, the cops knew we were up to no good, but they could never pin anything on us. I lost count of the number of times they raided my house—but they never found anything. No cash, no drugs, nothing. We kept that side of the business at arm's length. We had safe houses all over the place with wannabe gangsters holed up in them doing the risky stuff."

"So how did they finally catch up with you?"

"Ha! You wouldn't believe me if I told you."

"Go on."

"I pranged the car. Or rather, someone pranged me. Had to put it into the garage. The bastard cops set the whole thing up. When it was in getting fixed, they only went and fitted a hidden camera in the dashboard."

"They can do that?"

"Yeah. Who knew?"

"So they caught you in the act?"

"Yeah. But they waited a few weeks. Let the evidence build up. By the time they lifted me, they had hours of footage."

"Wow. Sounds like something you'd see in the movies."

"Yeah. But they had so much more than that. They had been following me for months. Had loads of footage of me buying burner phones from Tesco, picking up cash, making deliveries when we were a man down. All that good stuff."

"Shit."

"They didn't really have to interview me. They just played me all of the footage, and my solicitor told me to admit everything."

"Shit."

"Yeah. Shit happens, mate. You've just got to get on with it. Nothing else for it. I lost everything when I came in here. The house, my cars, the women—all gone. But I'll get them back. Just you watch me."

I didn't doubt Gary for a second.

Dry Socks

The newspaper's office hours were dictated by the unyielding prison regime. The system demanded that prisoners were on their wings at specific times of the day so they could be counted and accounted for. To facilitate this, the lads would be escorted back to their wing at 11:30 for lunch and returned to the office at 1:30 for the afternoon shift.

With two hours to kill over lunch, Sally would head home to walk her dog, leaving me to my own devices. While a two-hour lunch break might seem like a luxury, my options for doing anything other than work were limited. Not being a keyholder, I could either choose to stay locked in the office or leave with Sally.

If the weather was nice, I'd take the opportunity to get my steps in—walking around the prison walls or down to the beach to watch the RAF jets fly by. It was on one of these walks that I decided to doorstep Jimmy at his makeshift camp outside the prison grounds.

It turned out Jimmy didn't 'like it here' at all. He just had nowhere else to go. He did, however, like to talk—in short, rapid bursts.

"There's an old lady. She feels sorry for me. Religious old bird. Harmless. I think she's lonely."

Jimmy pointed towards his gas stove, where a pan of stew was slowly heating through.

"She comes down here most days with something to eat. Says I remind her of her boy. Died in Afghanistan. Beef stew and dumplings today. Better than anything I got fed in there."

"Why are you here, Jimmy?"

"Where else would I go?"

"No family?"

"Nope. Maybe up north. But they haven't spoken to me in years. I've given up trying."

"So why here?"

"This is where they took me. Finished a three-year stretch. Drugs. Do you know how much support you get when you leave a place like that? They give you a pep talk. Tell you not to come back. Give you a train ticket. I had nowhere to go. Oh, and £82.39. What can you fucking do with £82.39?"

"So you just stayed here?"

"Yeah. Spent the first two days living in a bush. On the third day, Sally—you know her, course you do—she gave me a tent."

"But why do you stay here?"

"Listen, I'm an addict. Clean now, but I'm still an addict. The council offered me a bed in a hostel in Cragsholme. Those places are just full of people like me. Junkies and other useless cunts. I'd have been straight back on the gear and right back on the wing in no time. I'm better off here. Living like the animal that fucking place turned me into."

Jimmy looked towards the prison, where a queue of visitors was beginning to form outside.

Some of them looked completely broken—shamed and exhausted by the trauma of visiting a loved one inside. Others looked much more upbeat, dressed like they were heading for a day at the races or a big night out on the town. Kids ran up and down the line, excited by the prospect of seeing their dads for the first time in months—or maybe by the opportunity of making new friends in the visitor centre's soft play area.

"So what do you do all day?"

"I remind everyone that the system is broken. There's no rehabilitation in that place. I went in there with nothing and left with even less. Well, £82.39 and a free ride to Cragsholme station. I mean, what the fuck? It's like they want you to fail. I'm here to show the world what that failure looks like. My name is Jimmy, and I'm a fuck-up."

"How old are you, Jimmy?"

"If I make it through the winter, I'll be 57 next birthday."

The warmth of summer was already a distant memory.

"You can't stay here forever, Jimmy."

"That's what the Governor says. Says I make the place look scruffy. But I'm a product of his regime. He made me what I am today. I'm his bastard offspring. He hates that people see his failings when they see me sitting here. But he can't do a thing about it. His jurisdiction ends on the other end of that sign."

Jimmy pointed towards the prison car park entrance.

"It's a small win—but I'll take it."

I liked Jimmy. He was as mad as a box of frogs but also seemed to possess a great wisdom. I made a point of visiting him every couple of weeks, enjoying his caustic appraisal of the prison system.

I always made a point of asking if he needed anything. He only ever asked for one thing.

"Socks. Dry socks. Can't have too many socks. Get wet socks and you're cold all day. Fucking cold."

"No, I mean, do you need any help?"

"Dry socks will help."

Over the next couple of months, I bought Jimmy so many pairs of socks that the staff at my local Marks & Spencer would nudge each other and laugh every time I walked into the store. God only knows what they thought I was doing with so many pairs of socks.

I never did write about Jimmy in *The Hard Times*, but I'll admit to occasionally channelling his voice when writing my more scathing editorials.

Dry socks couldn't save Jimmy. He didn't make it through the winter and was found dead in his tent two days before his 57th birthday. He did, however, prove the Governor wrong one last time. HMP North Shore looked just as scruffy with or without his little orange tent pitched outside its grounds.

Another small victory for Jimmy.

The Lynx Effect

Mondays were always a big day at *The Hard Times*. Not only did it mean the lads could put the boredom of two full days banged up behind them, but after putting the previous edition to bed on Friday, it also marked the start of a brand-new paper. But the real highlight of the day was the editorial meeting.

On the first Monday of each month, that meant a visit from our publisher, Bev.

Bev was a tough old bird. A fairly robust woman approaching her mid-seventies, she wore her prison keychain, belt, and pouch with the confidence of a seasoned screw. I swear to God, she walked like she had balls. There were some hard men here in HMP North Shore, but I never met anyone scarier than Bev.

However, Bev wasn't the main event at our editorial meetings. She was often joined by Andrea, *The Hard Times*' advertising rep and collective office wet dream.

The lads really made an effort on the days Andrea visited. At times, the stench of Lynx Africa could be overwhelming.

Mike, in particular, was smitten by her presence.

"C-c-c-c-c."

"I'd love a coffee, Michael. White, no sugar, please."

"B-b-b-b-b-b."

"Oh no, thank you, Michael. No biscuits for me. I'm going on holiday next week. You don't want me to burst out of my swimming costume, do you? Nobody wants to see that."

I could think of a newsroom full of men who definitely would.

Sure, Andrea was pretty. But she was also pretty odd.

"I do love coming here, Euan. You are so lucky to work here full-time."

"Really?"

"Yeah. I'd love to spend more time with the boys. In fact, I'd love to be actually locked up with them. Can you imagine? No responsibilities, three meals a day, free gym membership, and surrounded by all those fit lads. Has Tony got a girlfriend?"

"Andrea!"

"What? I mean, he's so strong but vulnerable. What girl wouldn't have their head turned by such a brute?"

"Jesus Christ! Have you sold any ads this week?"

Surprisingly, *The Hard Times* always carried a decent amount of advertising. Much of the ad space was taken up by legal firms, charities, and non-profits offering advisory and support services to the prison population. We also carried adverts for more progressively minded companies keen to promote training and work opportunities for offenders as they approached their release date.

As strange as she was, Andrea had her finger on the pulse of the prison news agenda and regularly came up with feature ideas that would interest readers and attract more advertising spend. Bev loved her commercial nous but didn't trust her with the men.

"Keep an eye on her, Euan. She's like a fucking cat in heat. Loves a bad boy. Fucking soft in the head sometimes."

The newsroom was always on its best behaviour when Bev and Andrea visited. But within minutes of them leaving, the air would turn blue.

Sally would give them five minutes or so to let off a little steam before reminding them of her presence.

"Gentlemen, please. Can I kindly remind you that there is a lady present? That's someone's daughter you are mentally molesting there. This isn't the VP wing, is it? I could arrange for some transfers over there if anyone is interested. Now, behave yourselves."

"Sorry, miss."

Everything Changes

The unpredictable nature of prison life meant that our little team was constantly changing.

Any misbehaviour on the wing would result in the Governor terminating their employment. He was of the opinion that working for *The Hard Times* was a privilege, and for once, the lads were 100% in agreement with him. Losing their job on the newspaper would be a significant blow. So it was always surprising when someone was let go.

"Mike, what's happened to Billy this morning?"

"B-B-Billy? Governor's let him go."

"Why?"

"F-found a t-tattoo gun in his p-p-pad last night."

"Where the fuck did he get a tattoo gun from?"

Oliver interjected.

"Made it from an old biro. You basically—"

"Don't want to know, mate. What the fuck was he thinking?"

Billy was a real asset to the team. As our head designer, he was honestly one of the most creative people I had ever worked with. But his creative spirit was accompanied by an artist's temperament—which was precisely how he'd ended up here in the first place. He didn't like playing by the rules. Didn't think they applied to him. And when he had a drink in him, violence became his creative medium of choice.

Back on the wing, the only thing he'd be creating now would be more problems for me.

"M-m-m-might not be a g-good time to tell you this. D-d-d-Daniel is leaving us n-next week as well."

Finally, some good news.

I genuinely liked most of the guys on the team, but Daniel creeped me out. To be blunt, he was fucking strange.

"What's the story, Daniel?"

"I'm sorry, sir. I should have told you sooner."

Daniel had no concept of personal space. Before I knew it, he was on my side of the desk with his arm around my shoulder, his face *literally* inches from mine.

He spoke quietly.

"I'm being transferred to a nick down south. You see, there's a special course I've got to go on before I'm eligible for parole."

I somehow knew I'd regret asking my next question.

"What kind of course?"

"Well, we're good friends, aren't we, sir? I mean, I know you're the boss here and all that, but I do count you as one of my very good friends."

"...Okay."

"Well, as friends, you have no reason to be scared of me because I'm not a threat to you."

"Glad to hear that."

His grip around my shoulder tightened.

"But if I was in a relationship with you... well, let's just say, I'd be *very fucking dangerous*."

Silence.

His grip loosened.

"So, I'm off to London to learn how to be a better boyfriend. It's the only prison in the country that runs this course, so I've got to go. I hate to leave you in the lurch, but for the sake of my next relationship... well, let's just say it's for the best."

"...Right."

The office door suddenly opened.

"Line up, lads. Time to get you back to the wing."

The office clock said 11:20.

"Bit early, aren't you, sir?"

Not early enough, I thought.

Daniel never came back after lunch.

I later learned that Gary, noticing how freaked out I was by the encounter, had had a brief word with him on the way back to their respective wings and somehow persuaded him to take the rest of the week off to prepare for his course.

It was good to know that one of the more level-headed lads had my back. Despite this, I feared I might have just opened an account—and be running up a prison debt.

The Recruitment Process

Recruiting staff for the paper was a long and protracted process.

Whenever possible, we recruited directly from North Shore's population, but at times, finding an offender who could write their own name—let alone string together a coherent sentence—was a big ask.

We advertised open positions in *The Hard Times*, which guaranteed a captive audience across the prison estate, and often received handwritten CVs. Occasionally, these were scrawled in felt-tip pen or crayon, with all manner of "careers" listed under previous experience. Brief telephone interviews were snatched whenever possible, with the noise of the wing providing a chaotic backdrop. But even when we found the perfect candidate, securing a transfer wasn't always possible.

When the stars did align, the candidate's first day at work was often our first chance to meet them. If they could stick it out for the first week, they'd usually stay on the team for a while. Many didn't last that long, so we were constantly recruiting.

Billy's replacement on the design desk could have given Alex a run for his money in the HMP North Shore *Businessman of the Year* awards. Graham wasn't a crook as such. He was an accountant by trade, handling the books for a number of dodgy firms in and around Liverpool.

He found himself in North Shore purely by being too good at his job—and in the wrong place at the wrong time.

"It's quite a funny story, really. I walked into one of my clients' offices just as he was being led out the door in cuffs."

"And you were lifted?"

"Yeah. But not immediately. They seized my laptop and let me go. I really didn't know what was happening or what to do, so I just went home."

"So what happened then?"

"Nothing. Not for another two weeks, anyway. Then my front door was kicked off its hinges in the middle of the night."

"Fuck!"

"Scared the shit out of me, but my wife was ready. She lunged at the first copper through the bedroom door. Stark naked, she was. I can still see her arse. Horrible. Poor bugger's probably still got PTSD."

Graham's laptop forensically documented every supplier, dealer, client, and movement of goods and money for one of Merseyside's biggest gangs. He'd also been diligently working on a detailed business plan that would see his employers expand operations into Manchester and Glasgow.

Not only had Graham landed himself in a load of trouble, but he'd also opened up a few new lines of enquiry. His meticulous notes introduced the police to several significant people of interest who had previously flown under the radar.

"The judge didn't know whether to thank me or send me down for eight years. To be honest, I'm glad he opted for the second option. My wife was furious about our front door, and I got the chance to do a graphic design course here in prison. I never wanted to be a bloody accountant anyway. I can't get into trouble drawing pictures, can I?"

"Hey Graham. C-c-can you draw me a m-m-map of w-where T-T-Tony has hidden his money?"

"FUCK OFF, MICHAEL! THERE IS NO MONEY!"

Day Release and Dance Moves

"Do you want a coffee, mate?"

It was Harry.

"Where's Mike?"

"Oh, he's not coming in today. Asked me to look after you."

"Is he sick?"

"No, he's having a day out."

I laughed at the absurdity of the idea.

"No, seriously. He's going out for the day—learning how to make the smooth transition back into society."

"You're shitting me?"

Sally joined the conversation.

"No, he's telling the truth. Mike's coming up for parole in the next year or so, so they like to get them back into the swing of things—get them out on the street to acclimatise. Right now, he'll be walking around Cragsholme with an officer, dressed in his best tracksuit."

"Like a date?"

"Yeah, but with absolutely no prospect of any funny business. Over the next few months, as he builds up confidence, he'll maybe grab a coffee in a café, visit the post office and buy some stamps, even shop for a simple meal at the supermarket."

"Is that really necessary?"

"You wouldn't believe how out of touch these guys are when they finally get out of here. Just listen to Oliver when he talks about clubbing and all the raves he's going to when he gets released. He still thinks he's 19 and has no idea how much the world has moved on without him."

"Hey, Sally! I've still got the moves. Just you wait until those chicks get a load of this on the dancefloor."

Within seconds of Oliver standing up and shaking his hips, Tony was on him, knocking him to the floor.

"Come on, pretty boy. Give Tony a kiss."

"Fuck off, Tony. Fuck off."

They wrestled like their lives depended on it, until Oliver lost his advantage, had his arms pinned to his sides, and grudgingly accepted a big, wet kiss on his forehead before breaking free.

The office roared with approval.

"You sexy bastard. You loved it, didn't you? You sexy fucking slaphead."

Oliver slunk back to his desk, wiping Tony's kiss from his bald head.

"Bastard."

From Hooligan to Health Editor (Sort Of)

Adam joined our little team after securing a transfer from Luton. He had the dubious claim to fame of being banned from every football ground in the UK.

"I'm not proud of what I've done. Well, I am. I mean, at least I've done something with my life."

In terms of life goals, I wasn't sure if getting five years for an incredible bout of violence—culminating in headbutting a police horse—would be at the top of many people's bucket lists.

Adam lived and breathed Millwall.

Officially, he was our sports, health, and wellbeing editor, but that sounded like a "load of bollocks" to Adam.

"I'm a football writer first and foremost. The rest of it is all shit."

He told me his entire life story within five minutes of meeting him. In that time, he went through the full range of emotions—from soaring highs to sobbing his heart out.

"I've had a shit few years. Lost my younger brother two years ago. I held his hand when he slipped away. Fucking cancer. Wasn't like me. Had it all. A good job. Lovely family. Even though I was older than him, I really looked up to him. That's when I went off the rails, really. Started fighting again in my fucking fifties. Mad, isn't it?"

I nodded in agreement.

Adam started his career as a hooligan at a young age.

"Looking back at it now, people might say I was groomed. I think I fucking was. But I wouldn't change a thing."

"Groomed? Like a..."

"Listen. Nobody tried to fuck me or anything. They looked after me. Taught me how to fight. Like brothers, really."

"So how old were you?"

"Twelve. I was a loner. Didn't have any friends."

Harry laughed. "You still don't, you Millwall cunt."

Adam ignored him.

"I started going to games by myself. Home and away."

"At twelve?"

"Yeah. I used to pay my 25p or whatever it was and go stand by myself. You've got to understand, back then you had to fight your way out of a football ground."

"When are you talking? The 1980s?"

"Nah. The seventies. Really fucking brutal times. Anyway, we were playing Oldham and these two massive blokes cornered me. I knew I was going to take a kicking, so I threw a punch first. A really fucking lucky punch. Floored one of the bastards."

"Really?"

"Yeah. Went down like a sack of spuds. So I was getting ready to take a beating from the other lad when Millwall came to my rescue. They couldn't believe I'd knocked the guy out. I was carried out of the ground on their shoulders and never went to a game alone again."

Adam could have talked and written about Millwall all day. The only problem was we didn't cover league football in *The Hard Times*. It was considered too divisive for a prison audience who didn't need an excuse to start a fight. Instead, Adam spent his day moaning about having to write about the limited provision of sport in prison.

"Chess isn't a fucking sport. And as for bridge—I'm only interested if you're talking about Stamford Bridge. We had some right good rucks there."

I could feel my eyes rolling to the back of my head. He was so predictable.

"The fucking Governor wants me to write about yoga. He goes on holiday to fucking Goa, gets a hard-on for some daft bitch in a pair of yoga pants, and now he wants me to write about yoga. He can fuck off."

Unfortunately, the Governor wouldn't fuck off and was constantly on Adam's case to broaden his output.

A Big Day Out Time Travelling

"How was your day out, Mike?"

He looked down at me, a steaming cup of coffee in his hand and a rare smile on his face.

"S-s-sweet. Really enjoyed it."

Mike spent the rest of the morning shift regaling anyone with the patience to listen to his stuttering review of his walk around Cragsholme. The highlight of his day? The car ride to and from the prison.

"I-I-I haven't been in a c-car for s-s-such a long t-time. I was s-s-shitting myself. H-h-holding on for m-m-my life. Kept telling the c-curt to slow down. Bastard p-p-put his f-f-foot down."

He then went into incredible detail about all the old ladies buzzing around on little cars.

"Mobility scooters?"

"I-I don't know w-w-what they were. They w-were f-f-fucking mad. I f-f-felt like a t-time traveller, or l-like I'd just woken up f-from a c-c-coma. It was l-like the J-J-Jetsons."

"Hey, Harry, you should get one," Oliver smirked.

"Fuck off, Oli."

"So, things have changed since you were last out and about. How long's it been now?"

"F-five years, or thereabouts."

"It's madness how quickly things change. You don't notice it when you're living it, but stuck in here, it's like a time capsule. Things stand still, right?"

Mike nodded.

"You should write an article about it."

"I w-will."

Mike hurried back to his desk and started tapping away at his computer with urgency.

Sally looked over.

"I saw what you did there. Anything to shut him up. He's a lovely guy, but holding a conversation with him is just exhausting."

Fine Dining, Prison-Style

Bev and Andrea were back in the office for the Monday meeting.

Andrea was busy flirting with Tony when Bev came and sat on my desk.

"The Governor wants to see us both for lunch today. That OK?"

"Sure, Bev. Anywhere nice?"

"Fat fucking chance. Good job too. You look like a tramp. Do you even own a shirt and tie?"

The Governor's lunch venue of choice was HMP North Shore's "prestigious" training restaurant.

The restaurant was used almost exclusively by the Governor and his assistant. Occasionally, a passing dignitary would be treated to a steak dinner, expertly cooked by Sammy—a bear of a man who, bizarrely, could be trusted with a set of knives in front of a politician or a minor royal.

The training kitchen was located in the prison's management and administration suite.

As we walked along the corridors to the restaurant, Bev lowered her voice.

"See all these doors? There's a useless cunt behind every one of them, just counting the days before their retirement."

"So what do these people do?"

"Nothing. That's what I'm talking about. They're all ex-officers on final salary pensions. A few years before retirement, they get promoted to a management role on a huge salary and basically play a waiting game."

"Come on? Surely they must be accountable to somebody? Have targets or something?"

"You'd think, wouldn't you? But by the time anyone catches on to the fact they do nothing, they've collected their gold watch and are off playing golf on the fucking Costa del Sol."

"Bev! I thought I heard you scuttling along the corridor. Euan! Good to see you again. How are you, young man?"

It was the Governor.

We were ushered into a room that, from the outside, looked like any other on the corridor, but inside, it sparkled with freshly pressed white linen, silver cutlery, and neatly arranged condiment sets. There were six tables set up for service, but we appeared to be the only guests.

Sammy loomed at the kitchen pass with a ladle in his hand. The sleeves of his whites were rolled up, revealing two massive, hairy arms covered in prison tattoos. Some of them were clearly fresher and more artistic than others.

A waiter suddenly appeared, dressed in overlong black trousers and a baggy, poorly tucked-in white shirt.

"Hello, sir. Bev. Guv. Please be seated."

It was Billy, The Hard Times' former graphic designer and prison wing tattooist.

"Hello, Billy. You're looking well."

"Thank you, sir. Can I show you the menu?"

The menu wouldn't have looked out of place in any respectable dining establishment. There was a choice of three starters, three mains, and three desserts. The only thing missing was a wine list.

"And what would you like to drink with your steak, sir? Can I recommend a Ribena?"

The Governor insisted on making small talk before getting down to business.

"We're very proud of what we've done here. Sammy's cooking is unbelievable. We had Bart Sellers, the

Parliamentary Under-Secretary, join us for lunch a few months ago. Said it was better than any London restaurant he'd eaten in recently. And you know, those guys love their dinners."

Ever the diplomat, Bev cut the Governor's pleasantries short.

"So, why are we here?"

"Well, to enjoy the food. And the service, of course. You both know Billy, don't you? I wanted to give him another chance after that unfortunate incident on the wing. Sammy speaks very highly of him."

"OK?"

"But I also wanted to speak with you about some very positive data coming out of North Shore regarding prisoner rehabilitation. Turns out the lads we've had working on The Hard Times have some of the lowest reoffending rates of any other cohort of offenders. I wanted to pick your brains and figure out just why that might be—perhaps bottle your insight and share it with some of our other work programmes."

Bev inhaled deeply.

"What do they say about statistics and damn lies?"

"I'm sorry, what?"

"Listen. We are very selective with our recruitment process at The Hard Times. The lads come to us with certain skills that half of the prison population don't possess."

"Go on."

"Well, they can read and write for a start. Some of them even have a half-decent education."

"OK. But there has to be more to it than that. I mean, you should be really proud of what you've done with the newspaper."

"Oh, we are. But you've also got to realise that most of the lads on the team come to us a little later in their prison careers. Like everyone else in here—including some of your buddies in the offices along that corridor out there—they've been beaten and broken by the system. They're sick of what it's done to them and want a little normality in their lives. By the time they come to us, they've already made up their minds to change their ways."

"So what are you saying?"

"I'm saying the lads have done all the hard work themselves. We just give them the space and respect to make those changes."

"I think you're being too humble, Bev. You should take greater responsibility for your success. What can we learn from your experience?"

"If you think you can replicate the experience of the lads over at The Hard Times and transplant it into a job making concrete blocks or learning how to dig ditches for the railways, you're more naïve than you look."

The Governor's mood shifted.

"You don't do yourself any favours, Bev. We bend over backwards to support your work here, and you give us very little in return. You really need to start playing the game."

"What do you mean? You've already told me we're bringing down your reoffending rates. Seems like you should be speaking to the other employers here."

The conversation was clearly over.

"Would you like to see the dessert menu?"

"No thank you, Billy. I think we're done here."

"Actually, no, Billy. I'd love some of that deconstructed rhubarb crumble and a coffee."

The three of us sat in silence while Bev polished off her pudding. She waved Sammy over.

"That was beautiful, Sammy. But, you know, I don't see why you don't just put the crumble on top of the rhubarb."

"Sorry, miss. We're not that kind of establishment."

Before we returned to the office, I took the opportunity to catch up with Billy.

"You're looking well, Billy. Have you put some weight on?"

This wasn't an insult. Billy had the build of a junkie and really needed to bulk out a little.

"Yeah. Thanks for noticing. In all the time I've spent in the nick, I've never eaten so well."

"Do they feed you here?"

"Not exactly. But the Governor never finishes his meal. He thinks it's polite or some other bullshit. Let's just say those leftovers don't go in the bin."

"Better than the food on the wing then?"

"Have you ever seen a fat prisoner in here? Last night, we had a cheap hotdog sausage, some powdered mash, and a spoonful of grey-looking sweetcorn. It tasted of nothing. Worse than nothing."

"School dinners."

"If they served that shit to kids, they'd probably find themselves in here for cruelty. Last week, I swear to God, I was given an apple, and they didn't even bother to take the 'unfit for human consumption' sticker off it."

"The lads miss you, Billy."

"Yeah. I hear all the stories on the wing, and I do miss working there. But seriously, I don't miss being hungry all the time and having to spend all my wages on tins of tuna and Mars bars from the canteen just to get through the day."

High Emotions

As we headed back to the office, all hell broke loose.

Alarm bells rang out across the yard. Officers hurriedly attempted to herd groups of jeering, non-compliant men back to their wings. It was one of those tinderbox moments where anything could have happened.

Then something really did happen.

Bev suddenly quickened her pace as she saw officers rushing towards our little prefab unit. It was quite something to see the old girl move so fast. Emotions were running high. People were shouting.

I'll be honest, for the first time in a long time behind these prison walls, I felt a pang of fear.

The newsroom door was wide open. That was unusual. Prison rules dictated the men were kept under lock and key at all times. In normal circumstances, only Sally or another keyholder could open the door, and it was always shut and locked out of habit.

Sally was sitting outside, hyperventilating. A female officer knelt beside her, trying to calm her down.

Inside, the newsroom was in chaos.

Nothing was where it should be. Desks and chairs were overturned, computer monitors knocked to the floor, and papers scattered everywhere. In the middle of the debris, the news team were all lying face down on the ground, their hands folded on the backs of their heads. More officers than I had ever seen in the prison loomed over them, batons drawn.

An officer was knocking frantically on the office toilet door.

"Andrea! Are you OK? We're going to get you out. Don't worry."

Two more officers came running into the newsroom wearing full riot gear.

"OPEN THE FUCKING DOOR AND COME OUT WITH YOUR HANDS WHERE WE CAN SEE THEM!"

"What's happened here? ANDREA!"

The bathroom door opened slowly.

Andrea walked out.

She looked a total mess. Hair everywhere. Make-up smeared across her face. Tights torn. She frantically tried to smooth her skirt. At first glance, she looked distressed. Or maybe just flustered.

Was she blushing?

The two officers in riot gear ran into the bathroom. There was a sudden crash of riot shield hitting solid muscle, and one of the officers came flying back out, landing flat on his back—eliciting a huge cheer from the lads.

The other backed out slowly.

Then Tony casually strolled out of the toilet, pulling up his prison-issue tracksuit bottoms and lighting a fag.

"What?"

The officers rushed him—but literally bounced off him.

Before they could regroup to restrain him, Tony dropped to his knees, put his hands behind his head, and smiled.

While he would ultimately comply with their demands, they were in little doubt about who was in charge of the situation.

Bev reacted first.

"WHAT THE FUCK HAVE YOU DONE?"

"Leave him alone. He was looking after me."

"NOT HIM, YOU STUPID GIRL! WHAT HAVE YOU DONE?"

Bev grabbed Andrea's arm and pulled her out of the newsroom, onto the yard, through the gates, and towards the prison reception.

Through the barred newsroom windows, I could see them screaming at each other.

Bev didn't appear at all sympathetic to Andrea's apparent trauma.

The Fallout

With the lads back on the wing and Bev and Andrea safely offsite, Sally helped me try to restore the office to something that at least resembled a newsroom.

"I don't know why we're bothering, Sally. I'm pretty sure we've published our last issue of *The Hard Times* here at North Shore."

Sally said nothing.

"So, what actually happened?"

"I've no idea."

She looked exhausted, like the fight had been drained out of her.

"One minute, the lads were working away. And then, completely out of nowhere—BOOM! It just exploded."

"Who…?"

"I don't know who started it. Everything went flying, and I just hit the panic button. Next thing I knew, the tactical response group was here, and the guys were all on the floor. Well… most of them. There was a headcount, and we realised Tony and Andrea were missing. And, well, you saw the rest."

"Are you okay?"

"I'm—"

Before Sally could answer, the phone rang. It took a while to locate it under all the mess, but the caller was persistent.

It was Tinker.

"Well, hello there, Euan boy. You've had a busy day, haven't you?"

"What have you heard?"

"Enough to make your little rag and that little slut Andrea the biggest story in the country tomorrow. But don't worry—I'm going to go easy on you."

"Why would you do that?"

"Bigger fish to fry, mate. But you should know I've put in a call to the Governor. I'll be in touch."

I don't know what Tinker said to the Governor, but I'm guessing it was an urgent lesson in crisis management.

What happened next was surprising.

Under Surveillance

It was business as usual at *The Hard Times* the next day. Surprisingly, even Tony was at his desk—not cooling off in solitary, as I had expected.

The Governor even called in for a bit of a walkaround.

"I understand you gentlemen had a bit of an adventure in here yesterday. Letting off some steam." He paused, scanning the room. "Luckily, nobody was hurt, and that young lady isn't going to make any complaints. You've been very lucky. But you won't be so lucky next time.

"Remember—what happens in HMP North Shore doesn't always stay in HMP North Shore. If news of your little adventure ever gets out, you'll all be learning how to fix train tracks instead of sitting in this cushy office. Don't let it happen again."

He pointed to the CCTV camera in the corner of the office.

"I'm watching you."

Then he turned to Tony.

"I'm especially watching you."

Tony smiled.

"Thanks, boss. I appreciate that."

A Bit of Sport

Harry filled me in on the details a little later.

"It was just a bit of sport, really. Tony wanted to spend a few quiet moments with Andrea—you know, they've been talking on the phone when she calls in for the ad sales. Soft lad's properly loved up, and, well, she's as mad as a box of frogs. So, some of the lads agreed to make a little noise. Cause a distraction."

"Who?"

"Oh no, that's not for me to say. But let's just say a few lads in here won't be smoking shitty roll-ups for the foreseeable. Not for the next few days at least."

"What about the CCTV?"

"That piece of shit hasn't worked in years. If it did, we'd all be up on some charge—including you, mate. I'm not so sure you should be sneaking all that extra food in for the lads in your pack-up. Not that I'm complaining."

"And Sally?"

"Yeah, she's upset. That's not good. But the lads made sure the madness happened around her, not to her. She knows how much she's respected."

"You could have got us shut down."

"Not me, mate. I spent most of the riot lying flat on my belly with a screw's boot on my back. Adam had a good go at the bastards."

Adam grinned.

"Ha! Not felt so alive in a long time."

I was lost for words. I couldn't even begin to understand how bored these guys must be, wasting away in this jail. Why would they risk losing the only thing that resembled normality—for the sake of a bit of extra tobacco and the promise of an exaggerated story about a quick fumble in the office toilets?

"It was a calculated risk," Harry said with a shrug. "Besides, what happens in North Shore stays in North Shore."

I frowned. "What do you mean?"

"Listen, you know as well as I do that the Governor just wants a quiet life. He must be about the same age as me. Retirement's not far off. Probably got his eye on one of those villas I was looking at down in Portugal. He doesn't want anything getting out in the press and spoiling that for him."

"Makes sense."

Only, it didn't. Not really.

But one thing I was sure of—Tinker knew exactly what was going on.

Faith, Fasting, and Food

"You might want to keep out of Alex's way this morning, Euan. He's in a foul mood."

"Why's that, Sally? What's happened?"

"He's hungry."

"He's always fucking hungry."

"Ah, it's a bit different today. First day of Ramadan. He's fasting."

"What? Alex? Blond-haired, blue-eyed, Welsh, miserable bastard Alex is fasting? Why?"

"He's a Muslim now."

"Fuck off."

"No, seriously. He converted—or reverted, or whatever they call it—a few weeks back. Happens every year around this time. Loads of guys make the change."

"Really? Why?"

"Well, I'm not one to cast aspersions on anyone's religious conviction, but I've got a hunch."

"Go on?"

"Well, the local mosque in Cragsholme is very supportive of the prison's Muslim population."

"So?"

"Well, you know they can't eat until sunset or something like that. It plays havoc with the prison system, especially around meal times."

"Yeah. I can imagine."

"So, the mosque prepares packed lunches for the lads to eat in their cells at night. Apparently, the imam is an amazing cook."

"So that's why Alex is a Muslim? He's thinking about his belly?"

"Ha! I couldn't possibly say. But he's so hungry at the moment, the silly bugger thinks his throat's been cut."

I've always found the concept of fasting incredibly inspiring. It takes immense discipline and sacrifice to deny yourself even the simplest of pleasures, like a glass of water when thirsty. I'm not sure Alex had considered this when he discovered his newfound faith. I'm guessing he was more focused on the delicious biryani waiting for him in his cell later that night than securing his place in paradise.

You could see the rage building in him every time the lads were allowed out on the yard to enjoy a cigarette

The lads in North Shore took their religion very seriously. I don't know how many of them actually had any deep religious feelings, but virtually every prisoner attended one or more of the religious services conducted in the prison each week.

Being something of a cynical atheist, I figured this was just an opportunity to meet up with the lads on other wings, conduct a little business, move some "goods" around, settle scores, and catch up on prison gossip. There was so little going on in these guys' lives that gossip was like oxygen to them. It kept them going.

In many ways, they were worse than little old women, desperate to know who said what to whom. Unlike little old ladies, though, any overtly salacious gossip could result in someone getting a slap, a razor blade to the cheek, or a boiling kettle of water poured over them.

Others wanted to work the system, believing it looked good to parole boards if they found God while serving their time. I'm not so sure how well this tactic worked out for the brace of priests we had locked up in the VP wing.

While, for many, the weekly visit to the chapel or mosque was just a social experience, there were those who genuinely needed and benefited from a spiritual life. For some, the only way of escaping these walls—and perhaps the shame they carried—even for just a few minutes, was through prayer.

Don't Look Back

While I had always tried to follow an *ignorance is bliss* approach to my colleagues' previous "careers," that strategy quickly fell apart over the course of a few days.

Sally was unusually late meeting me at reception.

I'd flicked through an old issue of *The Hard Times* and worked my way through the notices regarding the movement of offenders and contraband that had made it over the wall in the last 24 hours—200 cigarettes, a few grams of spice, and a burner phone.

As I moved along the noticeboard, I came across a rogues' gallery of notable prisoners. Amongst the criminal kingpins, far-right agitators, and raving paedos, there was a very familiar face.

"Well, well, well. What the fuck are you doing there, M-M-M-M-Mike?"

It turned out Mike wasn't in HMP North Shore for stealing the petty cash or unpaid parking fines. He was a proper gangster.

The poster said it all in bold uppercase letters:

WARNING: AT RISK OF TAKING HOSTAGES!

"Morning, Euan. Sorry I'm late. I'm on a bit of a go-slow today. You OK?"

I jumped out of my skin. I hadn't even heard Sally enter the room—no mean feat considering the huge metal door she had to unlock to get to me.

"What's this about Mike and hostages?"

"Oh! That's been up there for years. I wouldn't worry about it. He's not that man anymore."

As we walked across the yard to *The Hard Times* office, Sally quickly filled me in on Mike's past.

"Mike was top dog in a drugs gang on some kitchen sink housing scheme in Bristol."

"Mike was a drug dealer? He told me he worked in a print shop."

"Yes, he did. It was a great little business to clean his drug money. You know, buy a load of paper and ink, do a few legit jobs, and a load more fake ones—run the drug money through your account as cash payments."

The idea seemed totally ridiculous to me. Stuttering, subservient Mike—a drug dealer?

"Anyway, a couple of lads who worked for him ripped him off. Stole a load of cash or pills or something, and he wasn't happy."

"Go on. So what did he d-d-do?"

Sally shot me a disappointed look—the kind she usually reserved for the lads when they let her down.

"Sorry."

"Well, nothing much happened at first. He let them think they'd got away with it. They started getting cocky, taking the piss. They thought he was weak."

"He was biding his time?"

"Yep. Long story short, he had a long-term plan. Rented a house on the outskirts of Bath for the sole purpose of teaching them a lesson. But first—and here's where it starts to get crazy—he grabbed them off the street, took them into the woods, and staged a mock execution."

"Shit!"

"Yeah. Made them dig their own graves and everything."

"I don't believe it."

"Put bags over their heads, pistol-whipped one of them to the ground, then put the gun to the temple of the other, pulled the trigger and everything."

"Empty gun?"

"No. The gun was loaded. He raised the barrel just before he fired. Deafened the guy in one ear."

"So what was the house for?"

"Oh, it gets worse. He took them both back there, locked them in the cellar, and basically tortured them for the best part of six months."

She couldn't possibly be talking about Mike.

"Oh, that's not the worst of it. He completely humiliated them. Kept them half-starved and then made them fight each other for food. His gang were even worse—forced them to give each other blow jobs at gunpoint, filmed everything, and sent it to their families and every little runt that ran their drugs as a warning."

"So what happened next?"

"Well, one of them escaped. Ran down the street naked, screaming for help, and the rest is history."

"Arrested and landed a job on *The Hard Times*."

"Talk about career progression. Quite a change, right?"

"Yeah. He didn't mention any of that shit on his CV. That's crazy."

Not Your Friends

"C-c-c-coffee, Sir?"

"Jesus! Mike. No thanks. Not just now."

Learning about Mike's previous life was precisely why I never wanted to know what any of the guys had done. I was honestly never able to look at him in the same way again.

While he never changed his subservient attitude towards me, I questioned everything he did.

Was his downtrodden routine legit? Or was he just playing a game—pulling the wool over my eyes to make me feel sorry for him?

Or perhaps the system had actually broken him? The fact that the lads had so much respect for him told me a different story. He was still as scary as fuck. He just kept it well hidden under a meek and mild façade. And he wasn't the only one concealing his true nature.

Tim, our much-needed replacement for Daniel on the website, had been with us for a couple of weeks. At first, I thought we'd bagged another weirdo. But it took me quite a while to discover he actually *was* a weirdo.

He was quiet at first but had gradually started to come out of his shell. This process was accelerated after falling victim to one of Tony's infamous *"Give us a kiss"* attacks.

"Sir, do you mind if I ask you a question?"

I'd given up asking the lads to call me Euan.

"Sure, Tim. What's up?"

"Do you mind if I do a quick web search?"

"Sure. You're the web guy—you've got the internet. You don't need to ask my permission. It's nothing dodgy, is it? No naked ladies."

"Don't worry about that, boss. I think he likes boys."

"Harry!"

Tim leaned in and spoke quietly.

"I want to see what people are saying about me in the newspapers. It upsets my mother, you see. I want to check if what they're saying is true."

It was an unusual request.

We didn't encourage non-work-related web searches, and as every keystroke was monitored, most of the guys kept their online activity away from their previous lives.

I looked to Sally. She shrugged her shoulders.

"Can't do any harm."

"Here, use my machine. I'll give you a bit of privacy."

Tim sat at my computer, tapped away for a few seconds, and then spent 15 minutes or so carefully reading a newspaper article.

When he finished, he calmly shut down the browser and politely thanked me.

"All good?"

"Yes, fine."

Tim showed zero emotion. He clearly wasn't bothered either way by what the article said. But curiosity got the better of me.

With the lads back on the wing for lunch, I pulled up my web history and clicked on the page he'd been so focused on. The headline told the full story—just like I always told the gang they should write their headlines.

TENANT SLAYS LANDLORD IN BRUTAL HAMMER ATTACK

It made for disturbing reading. It certainly wasn't *"fine."* This wasn't a moment of madness or a crime of passion.

Tim had murdered his 80-year-old landlord after inviting him in for a drink when he called round to collect the rent. He just wanted to feel what it was like to kill someone. He had been planning the event for months—procuring the murder weapon and necessary materials to dispose of the body online weeks in advance.

Tim had always seemingly had a good relationship with his landlord. He paid his rent on time, and the landlord kept the flat in good repair. They'd often share a coffee and a friendly chat. He had absolutely no motive for the attack.

His landlord was just in the right (*wrong*) place at the right (*wrong*) time.

He literally didn't know what hit him.

Reading the article flicked a switch in my mind.

Who the fuck was I working with? Did I really know anyone in here?

I suddenly cast my mind back to the one piece of advice Bev had given me before I started working at the newspaper.

"These people are not your friends. They are not even your colleagues. You are there to oversee them and get a paper out. That's as far as it goes. You're not there to offer them emotional support. Don't tell them anything about you. Don't tell them where you live, who your girlfriend is, or even what your dog is called. They might come across as your best friend, but you can't trust them. Don't let them into your life. If they spot any opportunity, particularly a sign of weakness, they can and will use it against you."

I'd read stories about how offenders had befriended lonely or naïve officers before persuading them to bring drugs, phones, and even weapons into the prison.

Harry had told me there was so much contraband on the wing that it couldn't possibly have all come over the wall. He reckoned more than half the officers were bent in one way or another. This created an atmosphere where the officers didn't trust each other, and as a result, the job became incredibly stressful—making them even more vulnerable to exploitation.

Had I let my guard down?

Every fucking day.

Was I being groomed? Perhaps.

That night, I sat in front of my laptop and Googled every member of *The Hard Times* news team.

It turns out that you really don't know anyone until you've read the judge's closing remarks.

Apparently, I had made friends with people referred to as *"evil," "calculating," "dangerous,"* and *"cruel."*

Even Oliver's story shocked me. He'd always been very open about his *"moment of madness"*—but the cold-blooded nature of his crime hit differently when I saw how it was reported.

Calmly walking into a crowded pub and coolly executing two men while they sat at the bar read like something from a low-budget British gangster film.

The first man's head literally exploded from the bullet that entered the back of his skull and took off his face.

The second man had time to run before taking a bullet to the leg, bringing him to the floor.

Oliver's gun jammed before the final shot, giving the man time to plead for his life—before it was taken.

I always knew that Oliver had a strong will. But to have the strength of character to do something like that without his anger making him lose focus?

Terrifying.

Could a man who admitted (to me at least) that he felt no guilt ever be rehabilitated?

I no longer knew.

I was probably overthinking things—a consequence of spending too much time working in an unusual and, at times, stressful environment with, let's face it, unusual and at times stressful people.

I just needed to get through Christmas and New Year. Things would look up.

A couple of weeks out of the office would do me the world of good.

Until then, I'd just have to grin and bear it—and try not to be too spooked by my fucking terrifying colleagues.

Hard Times at Christmas

Christmas at *The Hard Times* was a pretty bleak affair.

Sally had done her best to cheer up the newsroom with a small plastic tree and some paper chains. I'd also managed to sneak in some treats for the lads in the form of cheap, chocolate-filled advent calendars on the stationery order.

Most of the men took their time opening the little windows of their calendars, delighting in the daily micro-pleasure of the non-branded milk chocolate treats with their morning coffee. Mondays were a particular treat, with three small chocolates to enjoy. These simple pleasures reminded me of how little joy these guys had in their lives.

Alex, however, consumed his advent chocolate in one sitting.

"Life is short. Might as well go for it when you can."

He wore a smug smile on his face for the rest of the morning. The following day, he was as miserable as sin as the other lads savoured their chocolates. You could say that normal service had been resumed.

Keen to create as normal a workplace environment as possible, Bev negotiated with the Governor to throw a bit of a Christmas party in the office. This was to take place during normal evening food service and relied on the goodwill of a handful of officers to facilitate it.

Much to Harry's delight, this included one of the dog handlers, who added Barry the drug dog as his "plus one."

"I really miss my dogs. They don't care what you've done. They just love you. Like, unconditionally. I've never known a woman that meant as much to me as my old dog. I don't mind telling you, I cried like a baby when my daughter told me that my old Stan had been put down."

Tellingly, some of the lads kept a wide berth from Barry.

Bev thought it would be nice to bring a few of our freelancers into the office. Obviously, we couldn't invite anyone from other prisons, but there were a handful of writers who had finished their sentences and, after passing a security clearance, were allowed into the newsroom. We also invited a handful of advertisers, which helped balance the gender profile of our guests.

Bev knew that despite the previous incident with Andrea—who was nowhere to be seen—the lads would be on their best behaviour if there were women present. It also gave them an incentive to smarten themselves up.

While we encouraged our guests to dress up, the invitations contained a very specific dress code—particularly for our female guests. It wasn't so much a case of what they should wear, but what they shouldn't wear.

Cropped, low-cut, halter-neck and backless tops were not allowed. There would be no sheer or see-through blouses, and tight-fitting items like unitards were banned. Oddly, only one pair of trousers or leggings could be worn at a time, and skirts, dresses or shorts had to be knee-length or longer. Chunky jewellery, hats and headwear were all prohibited, and if you wanted to leave before the clock struck midnight (actually 7 p.m.), you wouldn't be able to check your wristwatch—because those were banned too.

"What's a girl to wear, Sally?"

"Well, I think I'll be going for that sexy, lesbian, prison officer chic look that's all the rage in the correctional institutions of Paris and Milan."

"You wear it so well, Sally. That keychain and belt really bring out the sparkle in your eyes."

"Ha! Well, it certainly matches the bags underneath them."

The catering for our party had more in common with a children's birthday do. Lots of own-brand cheesy Wotsit-style snacks, cocktail sausages, cheese and ham sandwiches, a traybake cake, and lashings and lashings of orange squash.

At first, it was a little awkward. Our invited guests stood like frightened rabbits caught in the glare of a car's headlights. Our ex-offender freelancers tried to integrate themselves with the current team but were viewed with suspicion or jealousy whenever they talked about life on the outside. Nobody wanted to speak with the officers, who stood anxiously by the door, perhaps looking for a quick exit.

In an attempt to liven things up, Bev had organised a brief Christmas-themed quiz. It was actually a stroke of genius. Each team consisted of an offender, an invited guest, and an officer, and it would be fair to say it was as competitive as any pub quiz night I'd ever attended. Knowing there would be a lot of competition for certain team members—Adam for his sports knowledge, and Oliver for being one of the best-read people I'd ever met—team members were drawn from hats and assigned cheeky but non-offensive team names. I'm not sure how *Saved by the Bellends* made it past the censors.

For those two hours in mid-December, there was no *us and them*, no *haves and have-nots*, no *good or bad*. Just a group of people making the most of what they had in their immediate environment. It seemed to me what Christmas should be about. And then those of us who could leave, did leave.

Gabe had borrowed a minibus from a local garage and drove us all back into Cragsholme, where we continued the party at a Wetherspoons.

A lot of drink was consumed that night. I don't think the usual patrons of the bar—day drinkers doing a bit of overtime for Christmas—had ever seen a bottle of port passed around the table (always to the left) with such enthusiasm or frequency.

Bev's ego was thoroughly massaged by her guests, who universally heaped praise on her as "totally inspiring" and "worthy of a damehood." She didn't disagree with any of these statements.

I'll be honest—I found the whole charade rather boring. As a hack frequenting the newsrooms of London, I was used to mixing with the *great and good* and had rarely come across a *do-gooder* who wasn't doing it largely for their own benefit. Yes, I thought *The Hard Times* was a positive initiative, but with the low operational costs of running out of a portacabin in a prison yard and virtually no real wage bill, I was also conscious that Bev and her family were doing very well out of *The Hard Times*. Had this opinion been formed by the more cynical views of Oliver and old Jimmy? Maybe. But their opinions were as valid as anyone else's, even if nobody would listen to them.

Just before last orders were called, a new face joined our little group.

"Ladies and gentlemen, I'd like to introduce you to Apollo. Apollo will be joining us next year and taking over from Andrea on our advertising team."

Apollo had a certain charm. You might describe it as *smarm*, but the advertisers seemed impressed by the cut of his jib. He had a plummy, public-school accent but gave the appearance of someone who was fairly affable and could speak with anyone. I'd seen a lot of these guys in London. He was as fake as the veneers on his teeth, which he flashed with a confident smile.

Bev heaped praise on Apollo.

"Such a smart young man. Got his degree from Durham last year. Been travelling since he finished there. Helped build a hospital in Kenya last year. Very committed young man."

As far as I could tell, there were only two things Bev didn't share with the group about Apollo that night. Firstly, he was Bev's son. And secondly, but nonetheless essential information, he was a complete arsehole.

I'd later learn a third thing about Apollo. He'd recently had his heart broken by a girl called Andrea.

The Hangover

Gabe was unbearable the next morning.

He was loud—louder than normal. His erratic driving found and hit every pothole.

"Jesus, Gabe. What's that fucking smell?"

"That's my new Christmas Magic Tree. Rather refreshing, isn't it?"

In my hungover state, the chemically enhanced stench of pine forests and mulled wine literally made me want to gag.

"Your mate Sally's a bit of a sort, isn't she?"

"I don't think you're her type, Gabe."

"She could lock me up anytime."

"She's gay, Gabe."

"I'd cure her."

"What would the wife say about that?"

"You can fuck the wife."

"No thanks, Gabe."

It wasn't just my hangover that made work the next day so miserable. All the guys seemed to be on a bit of a downer.

"You enjoy it last night, Harry?"

"Yeah, it was fine."

"Just fine?"

"Well, you know, it was a change. Bit of a laugh, really. But you know when you guys left, we just went back to the wing. I was so full of orange squash, I was up all night pissing like a horse. My pad mate wasn't fucking happy with me. Ugly bastard."

"But still, it must have been good to get out of the old routine for a while?"

"Yeah, but you know, sometimes I think it's only the routine that keeps a lot of us going in here."

"How so?"

"Well, take Christmas, for example. You see it as a welcome break—right?"

I nodded.

"Well, we don't really need a holiday in here. On holidays, we just spend even more time locked up because half of the screws are on the sick."

"What about Christmas dinner?"

"That shite. Christmas dinner is sold to us as a treat, but those cunts don't know how to cook a turkey. Not that it's a proper bird. Last year, it was as dry as the Gobi Desert. Fucking tasteless."

"What about family? You get visitors, right?"

"I haven't seen my family for maybe ten or more years. Sure, some of the lads get visitors, but that just reminds those of us who don't of how little we've got."

"What about the lads? I see the camaraderie in here. That must help?"

"Most of the lads I get on with are on different wings."

"Of course."

Mike jumped into the conversation.

"Y-y-you've got me and Al-Alex over there t-to keep you company. He'll p-put a smile o-on your face."

"Kick a fucking man when he's down. He's a miserable bastard."

Alex didn't take his eyes off his screen.

"I heard that."

"You were meant to. Do you Muslims even celebrate Christmas?"

"Sure. Why not? I'm hedging my bets."

With the final edition of *The Hard Times* put to bed, the lads lined up to be counted, patted down, and returned to the wing.

Harry clasped my hand, shook it firmly, and wished me a happy Christmas. It felt like he was saying goodbye.

I seriously had a lump in my throat. It wasn't so much that I felt sorry for Harry—it was more that I felt sorry for myself. I was heading back to a cold flat above a shop in Cragsholm. A place where I had yet to make any investment in friendship and, as a result, had zero plans for the festive period. A dry turkey dinner on the B-wing of HMP North Shore sounded like an absolute treat to me.

Gabe was waiting for me in the car park.

"Why so down, chum?"

"Oh, you know. Just the pressure of work."

"You heading back to London?"

"No. I don't think so."

"So what are your plans for Christmas?"

I didn't reply.

"Yep. That's what I thought. No arguments—you're coming to ours for Christmas dinner."

I couldn't say anything, so I just nodded.

"You're welcome, son. You're very welcome."

A Dry Christmas Dinner

I learned a lot about Gabe and his wife Sharon over Christmas dinner.

Sharon met me at the door and quickly took the bottle of wine I had brought as a gift.

"We'll have to hide that. You can take it home with you later. Gabe's been sober for sixteen years now. He doesn't like to talk about it, so I'd appreciate it if you don't look surprised when you see the strongest drink we have in the house is tea."

After the work's night out, I was pleased to learn that Christmas dinner wasn't going to be a session.

I think I'd already realised that Gabe was a bit of a people-pleaser, changing his personality to suit the people in his taxi. His gruff persona was obviously shaped by the typical passengers he ferried back and forth to the prison daily.

Sharon, too, wasn't half the battleaxe Gabe had portrayed in the car. It was very clear how much the pair loved each other. It was also clear that Gabe and Sharon were drowning in circumstances.

Sharon worked as a carer—a job she loved. The way she looked at Gabe, it was clear that caring ran through her veins.

"I don't do it for the money."

"It's a good job too because there's no fucking money in it."

"People need me, and that's enough."

It wasn't enough for Gabe.

"They take advantage. She's on a zero-hour contract. Doesn't know from one day to the next how much money she'll earn. She keeps offering to get her badge and do some taxi runs, but there's barely enough work in this town for me. There's no point in her sitting on the rank or waiting for the phone to ring. Besides, it's not a job for a lady. You should see some of the pricks I have to drive around all day."

He winked at Sharon.

"Hey! Who are you calling a prick?"

Alongside the thousands Gabe owed the taxman, the couple were struggling with a crippling mortgage.

"Our deal ended a couple of years ago, and the bank just dumped us because, well, I'm self-employed and Shaz is on such shit money. Really left us in the shit."

"Is there anything else you can do? You know, apart from the driving?"

"Sharon wants me to start delivering parcels for one of those online companies during the day. But do you know how much they pay?"

He didn't wait for me to reply.

"Pennies per parcel. It's barely enough to cover the petrol and wear and tear on the car, let alone a wage."

This could have been one of the most depressing Christmas dinners I'd ever attended—and that includes the Chinese meal I shared with a handful of similarly friendless freelance hacks last year in London. But surprisingly, dinner with Gabe and Sharon was one of the most joyous Christmas meals I'd experienced since I was a kid.

The pair of them had so many problems, but they knew what was important. They had each other, and together, they could cope with anything. This perhaps explained why Sharon was so concerned about Gabe's blood pressure.

The meal was a simple affair, essentially a big Sunday dinner, complete with a large bird and all the trimmings.

"I fucking love pigs in blankets. I honestly believe they are the reason for the season."

"Gabe. Euan might find that offensive. You know these media types. He might be Jewish."

"Bit fucking late in the day to ask those sorts of questions, isn't it, you dopey mare?"

"Oh, don't worry about me, Sharon. This is delicious."

After dinner, we sat and watched some moronic festive TV. The Christmas special of Ronnie Barker's prison-based comedy *Porridge* raised a couple of laughs.

"Ha ha. You can't escape from the place. You must think this is so stupid."

"Well, you'd be surprised how close to reality this show is."

"Really?"

"Yeah. On a good day, it's just a game of cat and mouse with the lads on the wing looking for small victories over the officers. There's actually a lot of humour in there. They've got the prisoners and the officers down to a tee. There's a Barrowclough and Mackay on every wing. And as for the Governor—well, that's just spot on."

"So who do you think Fletcher is?"

"Oh, there's a lot of Fletcher in Harry. I've often thought that."

Classic Christmas *Top of the Pops* was next.

"We had him in North Shore for a few weeks last year. All those millions in the bank and the stupid bugger ends up somewhere like that."

Sharon's eyes lit up.

"I do love him. Did you meet him?"

"Before my time, Sharon. The lads still talk about him though. Top bloke, they say."

Gabe looked agitated.

"He's a bloody queer, him. And would you look at her skirt? Might as well have not put it on."

"Isn't that Kelly what's-her-name? Gabe, don't you fancy her?"

Gabe flushed.

"I do not!"

Sharon nudged me playfully.

"He's so easy to wind up. You should have seen him when we went to see *The Blues Brothers*. Got himself into a right lather over some pretty dancing girls."

One of the advantages of attending a dry Christmas dinner at a taxi driver's house is the free ride home. I was back home and in my bed by 8 p.m.

Bad News

I was woken by my phone.

"What time is it, Sally?"

"It's early. Sorry. Listen, I've got some bad news."

"Are you OK?"

"Me? Yes. I'm fine. It's Alex. He's dead."

"Alex?"

"Alex from work."

"Shit. Sorry. Alex. What happened?"

"Suicide. They found him hanging in his cell late last night."

I was lost for words but had to fill the void.

"Why? I mean, was he depressed?"

I immediately realised that was a stupid question. It was his defining feature. But to hang himself—that was taking it to another level.

"He left a letter. It's addressed to you. The Governor has it, but he's made a copy. I'll ask his secretary to email it over."

"Thanks, Sally."

"My pleasure."

"Happy Christmas, Sally."

"Sure. Why not? Happy Christmas."

The letter was difficult reading.

Dear Editor,

I hope this letter finds you well. If you're reading it, you'll know what has become of me.

You should know that the decision to take my life wasn't a rash one. It had been on the cards for some time now, and there is nothing anyone could have done or said to change my mind. The prison shrink is just going to have to put this down as another loss. It's not her fault. She tries her best with all that talking therapy stuff, but at the end of the day, it's just a load of shit. I really was just going through the motions until I reached this inevitable point. Tell her I'm sorry if my death is another black mark against her name.

You might say that my time in North Shore was the final straw. It gave me the time and, bizarrely, the freedom to decide how my story would end.

You know that I've made many mistakes in my life, but I'm not a bad man.

I wound up here after a moment of madness. Sheer desperation, you might say. I thought I had already lost everything before I ended up here—my business, my family, my reputation, my dignity—all gone. But HMP North Shore took the one thing I never thought possible to lose. It took my humanity.

This is a cruel place. They strip you of your freedom, your identity, your sense of purpose, and then leave you on your own to mourn everything you've lost.

Some people can cope with this loss. Perhaps they didn't have too much to lose in the first place. I pity them.

I, however, don't need their pity. Pity is not a currency you can take to the bank or trade for love. It's just the way it is. I have nothing left to give.

Alex

P.S. On reflection, maybe I do have something to give. There is some tobacco in my office drawer. Make sure Harry gets it. He's been rolling his fags rather thin recently. Also, Oli said he liked my trainers. If he can bear the thought of wearing a dead man's shoes, they're his.

"Bloody fool. He only had two years to go."

Sally shook her head.

"You really don't get it, do you? But then again, why would you? You haven't been here long enough."

"What do you mean?"

"Well, think about old Jimmy in his little tent. What was waiting for Alex on the outside? Unemployment, bankruptcy, homelessness?"

"Wet socks?"

Perhaps she was right. There was no hope to be found in a place like this. Freedom wouldn't have solved any of Alex's problems. Not immediately, anyway. He couldn't see past that.

"Should we prepare something to tell the lads? A little speech. Maybe a memorial or something?"

"I don't think so."

I was surprised at Sally's response.

"How so?"

"The lads won't want to dwell on it. They've got their own problems to deal with. Their own demons. Their own mortality. Alex isn't the first colleague they've lost, and he won't be the last."

Of course, Sally was right. This wasn't her first rodeo.

I did, however, hand Alex's letter over to Harry and asked him to run it on our letters page. It was, after all, addressed to the editor, presumably for publication.

He read the letter in silence before reaching for his bequeathed pouch of tobacco and started rolling two cigarettes.

"Mind if I step outside for a smoke, boss?"

"Sure thing, Harry. Sally, can you let Harry out onto the yard?"

"No problem. Harry, can you roll one for me?"

"Already have done, Miss."

I watched them through the bars of the office window. They sat smoking in silence, their eyes following the smoke into the sky. It seemed like a poignant tribute.

Nobody ever mentioned Alex's name again.

Road Trip

My phone rang. It was Bev.

"Fancy a little holiday, Euan?"

"Sure. Where are we going?"

"Not we. You. You'll be going on your own."

"Why break the habit of a lifetime?"

"That's what I thought."

"So, where am I going?"

"A little trip down to Plymouth. There's a conference on offender training and employment opportunities. They wanted me to do the keynote or something, but I really can't be arsed with that sort of thing. Besides, Plymouth is a shithole. Thought you could do it."

"OK."

"Good lad. We'll get you booked into a nice hotel. Four-star. How's that sound?"

"Sounds great."

"Just don't make us look stupid."

Prison Theme Park

The hotel wasn't great. It was a former prison building and retained many of the fixtures and fittings as part of its sick theme.

The hotel reception staff were dressed in what I could only assume were vintage prison officer uniforms.

"Welcome to The Jailhouse Plymouth. How long have you been sent down for, sir?"

"Sorry?"

"How long will you be staying with us, sir?"

"Just two nights."

"Perfect. You'll be staying in Block A, cell number 23, up on the first landing. If you'd like to take a seat for a moment, I'll have one of our trustees come and help you with your bags."

There was a boxy-shaped chair next to the reception desk.

"You have a BOSS chair?"

"Yes, sir. It checks for hidden devices on, or should I say, in your person. Would you like to take a seat? If you'd like to give me your phone, I can take your photo."

"No thanks."

The theme park atmosphere was furthered when a porter, dressed in a green and yellow prison uniform, appeared.

"I don't blame you, mate."

"What's that, sir?"

"Well, I've only been here five minutes, and I want to escape."

The porter looked at me blankly.

There was a sudden buzz and a shriek of excitement. A teenage girl jumped out of the BOSS chair.

"Ha ha. You've got me."

She ran towards the reception desk, presenting her wrists, ready to be cuffed.

"This place is crazy. That will look so great on my Insta."

I turned my attention back to the porter.

"It's the uniform, mate. Only high-risk prisoners wear clown suits like that."

We walked a very familiar route to the wing. However, there were some very obvious differences.

All of the gates on the yard were open, and the space was filled with planter pots, shrubbery, raised flower beds, and water features. And I was pretty sure the heated drinks terrace and tennis court weren't original fixtures.

"The swimming pool and spa are over there on your left, sir. It's in the old laundry building."

Even the gym lacked authenticity, with what appeared to be a rumba class in full swing as we walked by.

As we walked onto the wing—lacking the stench I fully expected to greet me—waiters, all dressed as offenders, ran back and forth across the area once used for association, refilling drinks and delivering plates of food piled so high, the lads back in North Shore wouldn't have known where to start.

The noise of the wing was dulled by carpets, curtains, and soft furnishings. The furniture was modern, with a quality and comfort level above anything I'd seen—even in the Governor's office. There were no mismatched plastic chairs, and the derelict pool table was replaced with a beautiful full-size snooker table, complete with balls and cues.

The guests slouched around like they didn't have a care in the world. They probably didn't.

Two men appeared on the wing wearing gym gear.

"Beer?"

"No. I think I'll grab a shower first."

"Don't drop the soap, mate."

The fucking hilarity of it all. In fact, I think I might have been the only one not laughing.

None of these people were having the kind of nightmares I was still having after meeting Paedo Steve and Harley a few months earlier. There was no shame, trauma, or guilt felt in this place anymore. Although, I was sure it still had its ghosts.

I was dreading walking into my own little pad.

To my surprise, the room was much bigger than I expected. They must have knocked two or three cells together.

While the prison-chic theme ran throughout the room, comfort was clearly more of a priority here. The beautifully turned-down bed didn't disappoint, and the en-suite certainly had more appeal than a shit-stained bowl in the corner of the room.

"You'll be needing this, sir."

"What's that?"

"Your key card, sir."

"Ha! OK. These aren't standard issue back at North Shore."

"If you need anything else—extra pillows or room service—just hit the panic button, and we'll come running. Oh, and if you're interested, we offer a guided tour of our museum wing on the hour. Gives you a chance to see what life was like for the prisoners back in the day."

I didn't know whether to laugh or cry.

There was no mistaking the sound of the cell door slamming shut. That sounded 100% authentic. I reached for my key card in panic and opened and closed the door several times before retiring into the room.

I lay on my bed, pulled out my laptop, and tried to review my presentation. I was supposed to be speaking about businesses' role in offender rehabilitation, but something didn't feel quite right.

To be honest, I wasn't really focusing on my reworked version of Bev's "death via PowerPoint" presentation.

How the fuck could anyone sleep in a room like this? A room stained with the sweat, tears, blood, and snot of men who had done terrible things and lost everything.

No amount of soft furnishings and comfort could disguise that this room had at times been full of fear and violence. Beatings, rape, murder, suicide. I thought of Alex left hanging in his cell, his trainers neatly set aside for Oliver on his bed, a note on his desk. How low must a man find himself to do something like that? How many times had it happened in here?

There was no way I could sleep in a room like this. I decided to rewrite my presentation.

Going Off-Piste

"Ladies and gentlemen, I'm sure you are all very familiar with the incredible story of *The Hard Times* newspaper. Under the guidance of its formidable publisher, Bev—everyone knows Bev, right? This little newspaper has rewritten the story of how privately owned businesses can invest, not only in their own future, but in the future of the many offenders who have found themselves working for the paper.

I'm sure you're all aware of *The Hard Times'* outstanding reputation for training and rehabilitation. No other programme in the UK prison system has such low rates of reoffending. We've all seen the figures, right? The Home Office is certainly keen to talk about them. I really don't know how Bev does it. She truly is an inspiration.

Unfortunately, as you may have heard, Bev isn't able to join us today, but she has assured me that she's sent along a worthy substitute. Please welcome to the stage the acting editor of *The Hard Times*, Mr Euan, um, er… excuse me."

The MC looked over to the side of the stage in the vain hope that someone would remember my surname.

I walked onto the stage to muted applause and the sight of several people making their way to the door.

"I'm sure you've spent a lot of time over the past few days discussing the rehabilitation of offenders across various educational programmes and training businesses. I've heard some incredible stories and met some amazing people. However, I don't think we're doing enough. We will never see true rehabilitation in the system until that system itself has been rehabilitated."

I was met with blank stares.

"Listen, I had the pleasure of staying at *The Jailhouse Hotel* last night. Has anyone else ever stayed there?"

A few heads nodded.

"What a terrible place. Who thought it would be a good idea to take a building like that and turn it into a theme park? Last night, I heard guests joking—while tucking into their steak and lobster dinners—about prison life not being so bad. I honestly believe some of them thought the spa was an original feature of the old jail.

It all just feeds into the stereotype that prison is a holiday camp, that nothing needs to change. That, in fact, what prisoners receive is already too good. But in my experience, prison is all too often a cruel place, focused almost exclusively on punishment rather than rehabilitation."

I felt a brief moment of panic. Where was I going with this? Then, I channelled Bev—the way she put the Governor back in his box when we met him for lunch.

"In my short time at *The Hard Times*, I've had the privilege of working with some of the finest people I've ever met. Many of them have done terrible things. But thanks largely to their own strength and resilience, they've worked their way through their troubles and tried to make the best of a bad situation.

They are fed up. Fed up with being looked down on by society. Fed up with feeling sick and tired all the time. Fed up with the violence. They want to live a normal life—a normal life like the one that has been gifted to the vast majority of people in this room without them even having to ask for it."

I paused for breath.

"I'm under no illusion that the guys I work with in *The Hard Times* newsroom are the cream of the crop. For a start, they can read and write—that's not something everyone back on the wing can say. They also have the ambition to lead a normal life because they've seen what a normal life looks like. Many have come from good, decent families, or at least had people looking out for them. They just took the wrong path and perhaps need a little help finding their way back again.

That route can't be mapped out by forcing them to jump through hoops or teaching them, parrot-style, what the right thing is. It's shown to them by helping them understand what normality actually looks like."

At this stage, I really didn't know if I was making sense.

"Normality, for most people in the prison system, is being locked up in a cell for 22 hours a day with someone they might very well be terrified of. It's a place where weakness is exploited, and strength is mistaken for cruelty. It's a place where doing the right thing is a dangerous thing. It's a place where people are taught to know their place—and that place is firmly at the bottom of the heap.

How can we claim to have rehabilitated someone when we release them broken?"

Now I was on a roll.

"So what happens when these guys are let out? Let's forget for a moment the criminal records, the licensing conditions, the stigma of being an ex-offender—all of which make it near impossible for them to find a job, a home, or anything resembling a normal life. Can you believe we're actually releasing some of them into homelessness?

That's not normal. In fact, it's one of the cruelest things I've seen while working in the system. I know what I'd do if I were faced with the prospect of sleeping in a tent in the middle of winter in a place like Cragsholme. I'd be smashing car windows in the prison car park just to be sure I got a warm bed to sleep in. In fact, I'd probably go straight for the Governor's car."

A murmur rippled through the audience—some nods of agreement, a few disapproving tuts. Maybe I was winning them over.

"Every day at *The Hard Times*, I try to create a sense of normality. I respect the guys, and they respect me. It wasn't always easy. When I first took the job, I was shitting myself. But I've come to realise that my fear was nothing compared to the fear they live with every day.

I don't believe we do anything extraordinary at *The Hard Times*. We just treat people with respect. And when you treat people with respect, they begin to accept their worth and react accordingly. The question is—how do we make this the norm across the country's prison estate?

Well, I guess it starts with the people in this room."

It started slowly. A woman at the back of the room stood up and began clapping enthusiastically. Before I knew it, the entire room had joined her. In my moment of madness, I had obviously hit a nerve.

The MC re-joined me on stage.

"Well, thank you so much for that wonderfully passionate presentation, Euan. I think it's fair to say it wasn't what we were expecting, but you've certainly given us all something to think about. Now, does anyone have any questions?"

A single hand rose on the left-hand side of the conference room.

"Robert Tinker, *The Sunday Sun*. How can the general public have any respect for dangerous criminals—like your colleague Tony Francis—when he won't fully admit to the extent of his crimes or reveal where he's stashed his ill-gotten gains? £12 million, I've heard. He'd get a lot more respect from the public if he told the authorities where that money was."

I fobbed him off with the standard 'unable to talk about individual offenders' routine. Judging by the headline in the weekend's paper, he wasn't amused.

Love A Lag: Do-Gooder Demands Greater Respect For Criminals

Scandals, Secrets and Cover-Ups

Bev wasn't happy.

"You! In here. Now."

She pointed towards our storage cupboard–slash–meeting room and marched me over with great urgency.

"About that headline. I'm sorry."

"I couldn't give a fuck about that headline. Tomorrow's fish and chip paper. We've got bigger problems."

I said nothing, waiting for the bomb to drop.

"She's fucking pregnant."

"Who?"

"Princess fucking Diana. Who do you bloody think? Fucking Andrea."

"OK."

"What do you mean, OK? It's about a million fucking miles away from being OK."

It suddenly dawned on me.

"Is it...?"

"His? Yes, it bloody well is. And she's keeping it. Stupid girl. Says she's going to tell him when she visits next week. If this gets out, we're fucked."

At that moment, I didn't realise just how fucked.

"I've got a meeting with her father tonight. We'll get it sorted. No other option."

Bev sensed I still hadn't twigged onto the scale of the problem.

"You do know who her father is, don't you?"

"No."

"For fuck's sake. You call yourself a journalist? Her name is Andrea Sellers."

I shook my head.

"She's Bart Sellers. MP for Cragsholm North and Parliamentary Under-Secretary of State for Prisons' daughter, you bloody idiot."

"Oh."

"That's right. Oh!"

"Where are you meeting him? Would you like me to come?"

"We're having drinks at his golf club. And no, they wouldn't want a scruffy bastard like you there. I don't need to tell you this—nobody finds out about this!"

As we left our little meeting room, a huge cheer broke out. Tony was sat on top of Mike.

"Come here, you sexy bastard! Give Uncle Tony a big kiss."

"Jesus, Tony! Get a room."

Bev left in such a hurry, she completely forgot Apollo, who was visiting the office for the first time.

"Sally, darling?"

Sally looked up from her screen.

"First things first. Don't you fucking dare call me darling again, son. You can call me Sally, or you can call me Miss. Nothing else. Now, what can I do for you?"

Apollo took a step back, clearly not used to his charm being thrown back so aggressively.

"Beverly seems to have left without me. Can you give me a lift into town?"

"I'll happily escort you off the premises, but only as far as reception. Euan, love, give him Gabe's phone number."

"Anything for you, darling."

She blew me a kiss.

"Haven't you forgotten something, Apollo?"

"No, I don't think so."

"What about ad sales this week? Anything else need to go in the paper?"

"Umm. No. Nothing extra this week."

"Well, thank God Andrea sold all those package deals before she left."

Apollo had barely been in the office for ten minutes and had already learned where he was on the pecking order

Sally later filled me in on the real reason she treated Apollo with such contempt.

"Listen, we all know who he is, but you've got to earn respect in a place like this. You can't come in and order Mike to make you a coffee—no pleases, no thank-yous—and then virtually throw it back in his face because there's no oat milk."

"He did that?"

"Yep. I think that's why Tony jumped on Mike. He looked like he was about to punch the stupid cunt's lights out."

"Seriously, where did he get his airs and graces from? I mean, his mother is as rough as a brick shithouse."

Apollo didn't leave a good impression on Gabe either.

"Who was that fucking knob I picked up today from your place?"

"Ha! Apollo. He's the new advertising sales guy. Or he will be if and when he pulls his finger out."

"He's a fucking ponce. Told me he owned the paper."

"Well, his mother does. He's just hanging onto her apron strings."

"Sounds like the pompous git needs to hang on a little bit tighter. I heard him on the phone crying to his 'mummy'. She was at home before she even realised she'd left without him. He was calling Sally everything."

"Bev wouldn't have liked that. She knows Sally is the glue that holds the paper together."

"Oh, she told him. I could hear her screaming down the phone all the way from the back seat."

Silence Bought

Bev was back on the phone the following day.

"So, I've spoken with Bart, and he's spoken with Andrea. It's sorted. She's going to stay with family in Spain for the foreseeable. Flying out at the end of the month—got a few loose ends to tie up first. Agreed to keep her mouth shut and stay well away from here.

We're both going to help her out with a bit of cash until the baby's born, and then I've got a few business interests in Marbella where she'd be an asset. She's a smart girl—knows what side her bread's buttered on. Needless to say, this goes no further."

With Andrea exiled to Spain and Tony tucked up in North Shore, who was going to find out?

Dodging Bullets

"H-h-hey, T-Tony, I saw your b-bird in Cragsholme yesterday."

"What's that, Mike?"

"A-A-Andrea. Saw her in the Post Office. I was b-buying a stamp. You know, as part of my reintegration pr-programme. S-she was p-p-p... p-p-p..."

My ears pricked up in absolute panic. Surely he wasn't about to let the cat out of the bag. Or, more to the point, the bun out of the oven.

"Come on, man, spit it out. P-p-p what? P-p-picking up a fucking penguin?"

I was willing him not to say *p-p-pregnant*.

"No. Some Euros f-for her hol-holidays."

It was like watching a car crash in slow motion—bracing for impact, only for the driver to swerve at the last minute. But then, just as relief set in, another head-on collision loomed.

"She was with that c-cunt Apollo."

Tony recoiled, the news clearly knocking the wind out of him.

"Never mind, m-mate. She, she looks like she's put on a few pounds. I still would, though."

Fuck. Time to intervene.

"Hey, Mike. How are you getting on with that feature I asked you to look at?"

"O-on it, boss."

"Tony. What are you working on at the moment?"

"Nothing at the moment, boss. To be honest, I don't feel so good. Mind if I take the afternoon off?"

Thinking it might be for the best, I agreed to let him stay on the wing after lunch. We might just have dodged a bullet there.

In reality, the bullet simply ricocheted.

Apollo's Paradigm Shift

With Andrea off the payroll—officially, at least—Mondays morphed into a pretty normal day. Only more disappointing.

Apollo was the main cause of my disappointment. Ad sales were clearly not his forte. In fact, his so-called charm and wit had resulted in a few contracts being terminated.

"I wish we could terminate him," Sally muttered.

"Careful, Sally. He'll hear you."

"And that would be a problem because…?"

Apollo talked a good game—if that game was *Bullshit Bingo*.

"I just haven't had the bandwidth to make the calls," he explained.

"What?"

"There's some low-hanging fruit I'm trying to harvest. We'll see a paradigm shift in the next couple of weeks."

"Jesus! Less of your crap. Just pick up the phone and bloody sell some ads."

To say the lads were lukewarm toward Apollo was an understatement. He was the only guest I'd ever seen Mike refuse to make a coffee for.

"Y-y-you know wh-where the kettle is," Mike told him.

"Instant? I'm not drinking that shit."

"In that case, you'll be going thirsty."

"What is this place?" Apollo scoffed.

"It's a fucking prison, not a bloody Costa, you stupid cunt."

"OLIVER!"

"Sorry, Miss."

Tony had apparently started block-booking therapy sessions on Mondays—the very same days Apollo was in the office.

Despite taking advantage of all the talking therapy on offer, he still had plenty to say when he arrived.

"Was that cunt in this morning?"

"I'm sorry, Tony. That's not the kind of language a lady wants to hear about one of her esteemed colleagues."

"He's a cunt!"

Sally peered at Tony over her glasses.

"He is, Tony. He is."

Doing The Business Behind Bars

Aside from the drop in advertising revenue, the first few issues of the year ticked by incredibly smoothly. The lads pulled together some incredible content, and I'll admit, I was very proud of the papers we put out.

With everything running so efficiently, it was sometimes easy to forget where we were. Most of the time, I felt like I was working with complete professionals.

The team was also growing.

Filip had recently transferred from HMP Liverpool, following a glowing recommendation from the prison's talkative education officer.

"Filip's been with us for nearly ten years, and I've never come across such a motivated individual."

Judging by press reports, he was certainly motivated when he arrived at Dover with £12 million worth of heroin in the back of his plumber's van.

"He hardly spoke a word of English when he arrived in Liverpool but was fluent within months. Spoke better English than most of the local guys on the wing, including the officers. Told me he had a system and could teach anyone to speak a foreign language in no time at all. He started teaching me Polish. *Dzień dobry.* Well, that's about as far as I got, but he tried."

After mastering English, Filip threw himself into the prison library, demanding a constant supply of books.

"They were all business books. He had a real flair for business. Took an Open University degree in Business Studies and just flew through it. He's an incredibly talented man."

He was also ambitious.

"He's a big fan of *The Hard Times*. Has always said he'd like to set up a similar publication back in Poland. He's due for release in about twelve months, and he'll be driven straight to the airport and deported. Be good if he can get some experience with your team before he goes."

Filip was a joy to have on the team. He wasn't like any of the other guys. It was like having another adult in the room. There was no banter with him. Just hard work.

Filip also had no interest in being a journalist. His focus was 100% commercial. He wanted to understand the mechanics of our operation—how we worked with printers and distributors, how we sold subscriptions and advertising, how we accessed government grants and other funding. He was all about the money.

I put Filip to work under Apollo's guidance. In reality, he soon took over the commercial side of the operation.

"Apollo, I think, is a very strange boy," Filip observed one day.

"How so, Filip?"

"He asks too many questions. Questions about things that aren't important."

"What sort of questions?"

"How to not get caught by the police. This isn't something I'm an expert in."

"Obviously."

"And how to clean money. He's very interested in that process, but he'll not learn that from me."

"Glad to hear that."

"I think he is very immature. He's not a serious man."

Filip was *so* serious, Tony insisted on calling him "Sir."

"There's no need for that, Tony. He's one of the lads."

"But is he, sir? He gives out serious boss vibes. I reckon he's after your job."

Man on the Run

I was woken by Sally calling my mobile. Experience told me this wouldn't be good news.

"Hey, Sally. It's not even six. What's up?"

"Mike's missing."

"What?"

"Gone fucking AWOL. Didn't report back to the prison last night after his little jolly into Cragsholme yesterday. It's all over the news."

I quickly tuned the radio to Cragsholme FM.

"So what do we know about this prisoner? Is he dangerous?"

"Well, the authorities will claim he is a model prisoner and totally reformed. But I would say Michael Peterson is a very dangerous man."

I recognised the commentator's voice.

"Bloody Tinker."

"He has a track record for extreme violence and, let's not forget, is in prison for taking and torturing hostages."

"So, obviously, the police are very keen to find this dangerous individual as soon as possible. How can our listeners help? Should they check their outhouses and sheds?"

"No, that's the last thing I would do. If I lived anywhere near Cragsholme, I'd make sure all my doors and windows were locked and I'd stay inside. Don't send the kids to school. Don't go to work. Phone in sick if you have to. Seriously, don't answer the door to anyone. This is a very dangerous situation, and there's no telling what Michael Peterson will do if he is desperate enough—and I believe he is a very desperate man."

It was like a crash course in tabloid journalism. Scare the shit out of your audience.

The presenter took the baton from Tinker and ran with it.

"Let's get this straight. Michael Peterson didn't escape. They've been letting this incredibly dangerous individual out every week to walk freely amongst the good people of Cragsholme for months now. What are they doing letting these, quite frankly, dangerous criminals out on their own and expecting them to simply return in the evening of their own volition?"

"God only knows. The blame for this goes all the way to the top."

"The Governor?"

"No. This goes all the way up to the very top—Bart Sellers, for a start, and maybe even the Prime Minister himself. Cameron has questions to answer about this."

"Questions I think many of our listeners will have, judging by how our switchboard is lighting up. On line one, we have Emma. What would you like to say, Emma?"

"What has the world come to? These prisons are like holiday camps. I know what I would do with them."

"And what's that, Emma?"

"Throw away the flipping key. Seriously, hanging is too good for them sometimes."

"You'll get no argument from me there, Emma. Coming up, more news on the North Shore prison break straight after this absolute banger from the eighties—*Hunting High and Low* by A-ha."

My phone rang again. It was Gabe.

"Your boy Michael is causing everyone problems today. Every road in and out of Cragsholme is blocked. It's taking hours to get anywhere. I reckon you'll be quicker walking in today."

"Thanks, Gabe. I'll take my bike. Been meaning to do that for a while. It's a nice day, so…"

"A nice day to sit in fucking traffic. Might as well write the fucking day off."

Gabe wasn't exaggerating. The normally quiet roads of Cragsholme were in absolute chaos. I cycled past miles of vehicles going nowhere while the police forensically searched every car, van, and lorry. They were even looking underneath the vehicles, as if Mike had the strength to hold on to the underside of a truck.

With my face in clear view, I was waved through most of the roadblocks with just a cursory glance and made it to the prison in good time. I felt good about myself. Gabe might have lost a regular fare.

The Governor met me at reception and quickly brought me back down to earth.

"Are you OK? You look like you're having a heart attack."

"No, Governor, just a bit flustered after a bike ride."

"Oh! OK. Well, never mind—much more pressing issues. No newspaper today. The office is closed until we get to the bottom of this. We can't have senior members of your team running around the bloody countryside. I need you to come up to my office. We have some questions for you. Sally and Apollo are up there already."

"Have they told you anything useful?"

"Apollo has been very helpful. He's a very capable young man. A credit to his mother."

High Stakes

"If anyone knows where Mike is, it's that Tony. They are, and please excuse the pun, as thick as thieves."

"What are you suggesting, Apollo?"

"I'm suggesting that Tony has told him where he hid his haul, and Mike has gone looking for it."

"Really?"

"I'd bet my reputation on it."

"So we're not talking really high stakes then."

"Sorry?"

"Get Anthony up here. Now."

The stakes were about to get much higher.

Vanished Without a Trace

"He's living in cloud cuckoo land, sir. There is no money."

"So you keep saying, Tony. Are we really meant to believe that?"

"There is no fucking money, and I have no idea where Mike is."

Sally leant across the table and clasped Tony's hands.

"Listen, Tony, love. If you know anything at all, you'll be helping Mike out by telling us. The longer he's out there, the more trouble he'll be in."

"I know, miss. And I really want to help you. I just don't know anything."

We were interrupted by the Governor's PA crashing into the office.

"Governor! Turn the television on. Quickly!"

"What's all this about, Tracey? We've got b—"

"Please, sir, turn the television on. You'll not want to miss this."

The Governor reached for the remote on his desk and instinctively flicked to Sky News. The face on the screen was instantly recognisable.

"Andrea?"

"Fuck me!"

"Turn it up."

"Police are increasingly concerned about the welfare of Andrea Sellers. The daughter of MP and Prisons Secretary Bart Sellers was reported missing after failing to arrive at a relative's home in Málaga, Spain, where she was expected to be staying on holiday. Reports suggest that Andrea missed her flight and has not been seen since. Police believe she

may have been snatched by Michael Peterson, who is currently on the run from HMP North Shore high-security prison."

"I'll fucking kill the cunt."

"Miss Sellers was known to the prisoner through her work on the prison newspaper—The Hard Times."

"I'LL FUCKING KILL THE CUNT!"

The Governor reached for the alarm button under his desk.

Two officers burst into the office. Tony knocked the first flat on his back before stepping away and raising his hands in surrender.

"I'm sorry. Oh, what's the fucking point?"

As he was led out of the Governor's office, I swear I saw a tear in his eye.

"He knows more than he's letting on."

Sally threw Apollo a look so sharp it could have drawn blood.

"Shut up, Apollo, you stupid boy."

Media Frenzy

For the next week, *The Hard Times* was never out of the headlines, usually accompanied by Tinker's byline.

The stories became increasingly critical of our little operation.

"Soft Times for Britain's Hardest Lags", "Woke Prison Newspaper Teaches Old Criminals New Tricks", "Hold the Front Door Open"—each headline more sensational than the last.

The central argument? That *The Hard Times* wasn't a vital tool in the rehabilitation of offenders but a glorified networking hub for criminals—a place where they could not only plan their next big job but also access the communication channels needed to put those plans into action.

This narrative contradicted every piece of data the Home Office had collected on our organisation. But since when did Tinker let the truth get in the way of a good story?

Damage Control

With *The Hard Times* temporarily closed, Bev put me to work on crisis management.

I was back in London, holed up in a tiny hotel room barely bigger than a prison cell, ferried back and forth by Addison Lee between newsrooms and studios. Bev made sure I faced every journalist who had questions about *The Hard Times*, Mike, and, of course, Andrea.

They were going to write about us anyway—better to have some control over the narrative.

In truth, we had no evidence that Andrea's disappearance had anything to do with Mike, but journalists love putting two and two together and making five. I was used to the game, well-practised at countering loaded questions with reasonable answers.

"What sort of man is Michael Peterson?"

"I've always found him extremely hard-working and polite. He also makes a mean cup of coffee."

"Can men like that ever really be reformed?"

"I like to think so."

"Some say modern prisons like HMP North Shore are just like holiday camps."

"Is that a question or a statement?"

"Is HMP North Shore a holiday camp?"

"I've never stayed at a holiday camp where you're forced to share a cell with a potentially dangerous individual and a stinking toilet for upwards of 23 hours a day. But then again, I've never been to Pontins, so I couldn't possibly comment."

The questions blurred together, an endless cycle of speculation and innuendo.

And then there was Andrea.

"She's a very pretty girl. You must be worried about her in this highly unusual situation?"

"I'd be worried about her regardless of her looks."

"Do you have any words of comfort for her father Bart Sellers?"

"No. I would have nothing to base those words on. I'm a journalist, and like you—I hope—I only work with facts."

"What do you think has happened to her?"

"Like I said, I'm not in the business of divination."

But not all my media colleagues shared my principles.

Mike's face was plastered across the tabloids and broadsheets alike, accompanied by words like "Monster", "Fiend", and "Ghoul". So-called journalists dredged up every old story they could find about his past as Bristol's most ruthless drug dealer.

Meanwhile, Andrea was painted exclusively as the innocent victim—an angel in the hands of a dangerous criminal.

The papers had raided her Facebook for suitably wholesome images. Despite the fact she'd been out of full-time education for years, they ran pictures of her in her school uniform, further solidifying her role in the narrative.

Then, everything changed.

The Scandal Deepens

"ONLYFANS?! ARE YOU FUCKING SERIOUS?"

Bev was on the phone, and she didn't sound happy.

"Did you know about this?"

I silently shook my head, despite the fact Bev couldn't see me.

"What am I going to tell Bart?"

Again, I had no answer.

"That poor man. First, his daughter is kidnapped by someone we should never have trusted…"

"We don't know that."

"…and now this. That stupid, stupid girl."

The photos of Andrea in her school uniform no longer looked so innocent.

"Where are you today?"

"I'm at LBC this afternoon, and then I've got dinner tonight with an old contact at *The Guardian*."

"OK, try and pour some water on this filth. Throw Michael under the bus if need be. God knows he's caused us enough trouble, even if he hasn't got Andi. Tomorrow, first thing, I want you back on that train to Cragsholme. I'll be in the office at 2pm."

"Oh. Are we back in business?"

Bev hung up.

Fact Stranger Than Fiction

Sally met me at reception.

"We're going to the wing. Bev's over there already."

"Why?"

"She's putting the thumbscrews on Tony. Although, between you and me, I don't think he knows anything."

"Have you seen the papers today?"

"It's all anyone can talk about in here."

"Yeah, that Tinker is a piece of fucking work."

"Do you really think Mike has kidnapped Andrea to get Tony to reveal where his stash is?"

"I don't know anymore."

"Did you know she was pregnant?"

"Yeah. Bev told me. But how the fuck did Tinker find out?"

"Is there anything he doesn't know?"

Paedo Steve and Harley stood outside the wing's office—Steve leaning on his mop, Harley clutching his limp rag and a can of polish. Their attention was focused entirely on the odd couple seated on the other side of the wing.

Tony was sobbing loudly, his 18 stones of muscle shuddering violently.

"I haven't heard a thing, Miss. I promise you that. I love that girl. And my baby. It is my baby, isn't it?"

Bev said nothing.

"Hello, Sir. Miss. Don't usually see you around these parts."

It was Oliver. He was leaning in the door of his pad.

"Fancy a coffee? I'll put the kettle on If you don't mind sharing a plastic cup."

"No, you're alright Oliver, thank you.. So this is your pad?"

It was a single cell, spotlessly clean and lined with books. A small photo of a young girl was taped to the wall next to his desk.

"Is that your sister?"

"Yep. The reason why I'm in here—and the only reason I would ever consider coming back. No regrets."

There was a brief pause while we contemplated Oli's situation.

"Fuck me, I'm bored, Sir. When are we opening the paper again? I've read every single one of those books three times."

Oliver nodded in the direction of Steve and Harley.

"Going stir-crazy watching those two idiots doing nothing all day."

"How's he been?"

"Tony? You see it all."

"Do you think he knows anything?"

"About Mike and his little girlfriend? Absolutely not."

"Would you tell me if you knew differently?"

"I wouldn't lie to you, Sir. I just wouldn't tell you the truth. But it doesn't matter—Tony hasn't got the emotional intelligence to keep a secret like that. He's heard nothing."

"What does your gut tell you?"

"My gut? What do you mean?"

"Your gut instinct as a journalist. What does your gut tell you?"

"It tells me that I'm sick of eating unspecified meat cutlets from that bloody canteen."

Oliver grabbed a book from his collection and flopped onto his bed.

"But I'll tell you something—fact is often stranger than fiction."

Good News

It turned out Oliver had a great journalistic gut, and the facts that were about to emerge were stranger than any fiction I'd read recently.

After days of what felt like constant abuse and ridicule in the tabloid press, my little catch-up with my old colleague at *The Guardian* finally paid off.

Instead of focusing on our rather public failures—an escaped prisoner, a possible kidnapping, and the daughter of a prominent MP falling pregnant to a violent criminal—it took a more positive view.

It highlighted our incredible rehabilitation record, our groundbreaking campaigns for prison reform, and the importance of creating rewarding work experiences rather than meaningless busywork behind bars. It positioned Bev as a visionary business leader and the Governor as a progressive force in the sector.

Egos had well and truly been massaged. It must have done the world of good.

Bev called.

"Hello, Euan, son. The Governor fucking loves us. We're getting the band back on the road. *The Hard Times* reopens for business tomorrow."

Hold the Front Page

It was all smiles as we welcomed the team back to the office.

"No time to chat, lads. We've got three days to get a newspaper out."

Without hesitation, the team headed straight to their desks, producing various scraps of paper filled with notes, half-formed ideas, and even fully written stories they had scribbled down while in their cells.

All morning, the office buzzed with the sound of fingers hammering keyboards and voices bouncing ideas off one another.

"You boys are fucking brilliant!"

The paper came together in no time. Filip had even managed to win back some of the advertisers that Apollo had lost. All that was left was to decide on the front-page lead.

Sometimes, lead stories are hard to find. Other times, they land in your lap. Today, luck was on our side.

The phone rang.

"Newsdesk. This is Oliver. How can I help?"

He listened intently.

"You're fucking kidding me."

Every eye in the office was on him now.

"Thank you."

Oliver threw the phone down with a clatter, then, with theatrical precision, slowly climbed onto his desk.

"HOLD THE FUCKING FRONT PAGE! HAVE I GOT A STORY FOR YOU GUYS."

He wasn't exaggerating.

Almost two weeks after absconding, Mike had walked into a pub on the outskirts of Cragsholme.

According to our caller, he had casually strolled in, ordered a double vodka and a bag of crisps, offered no payment, and taken them outside to enjoy in the sunshine while he waited for the inevitable.

He didn't have to wait long.

Armed police stormed the beer garden, barking orders, guns trained on him. Mike wasn't about to give them any trouble. He simply dropped to his knees, placed his hands behind his head, and surrendered without a fight.

Back on the Wing

"Gary! Did you see Mike last night? I assume he's on your wing now?"

"Yeah, he is. No, I didn't see him last night, but I caught him this morning getting some toast."

"How's he doing?"

"He's alright. Pretty badly beaten up and looks like he could do with a decent meal inside him. I'll tell you what—he fits in perfectly with half those junkie bastards on that wing."

"What's he saying? Any news about Andrea?"

"Says he knows nothing about her disappearance, and the police must be pretty convinced by his story, or he wouldn't be straight back here and on the wing."

"So what is his story?"

"Not sure, but I'll find out. He'll be on my wing for the next few days at the very least, so hopefully we'll get a chance to catch up."

Sally joined the conversation.

"When's he coming back to work?"

"I'm sorry, Sally, but I've spoken to the Governor, and that's not going to happen any time soon. Bloody shame, really. He makes a great c-c-cup of c-coffee."

Sally looked at me disapprovingly before cracking a smile.

"You poor lamb. Whatever are you going to do without him?"

"I don't know, Sally. He'll be hard to replace."

I stood up and theatrically scanned the room.

"Harry! You've been promoted. Put the kettle on, mate."

"It would be an honour, sir."

Hiding in Plain Sight

Gary was good to his word and came back with Mike's story.

"So, he was out on one of his visits to town. You know, doing the usual shit—buying a loaf of bread, opening a post office savings account, all that good stuff. Anyway, he was walking past the pub, and, you know, he really fancied a pint."

"Silly lad. If he'd come back here with any trace of alcohol in his system, he'd have been fucked."

"Oh, he knew."

"So, he had a pint?"

"He had more than a pint. He went to town. Got absolutely pissed."

"Where did he get the money?"

"I don't know. He's a resourceful dude, you know."

"Nicked a wallet?"

"Yeah, maybe."

"So what happened next?"

"Stole a waterproof jacket from the British Heart Foundation shop and bedded down with a couple of homeless guys in Boots' doorway."

"For two whole weeks?"

"Yeah, pretty much. Those guys can be fun if you like getting off your face. Know how to throw a party and all that."

"But the town was crawling with police looking for him."

"Yeah, useless cunts. But that's not the half of it."

"Go on?"

"Thought his game was up on the first morning he was out there. Bev and Apollo walked straight past him."

"Really?"

"Yeah. He's pretty sure Bev didn't clock him, but he said Apollo made full-on eye contact."

"You're kidding me?"

"Nah. But you know that cunt is so full of himself, he probably didn't... Well, God knows what's going on in his mind."

"So, you say he took a beating?"

"Yeah. That was the final straw. Some kids fell out of the pub after Cragsholme Town lost and wanted to take out their frustrations on some random homeless guy. So he took a kicking, decided the streets weren't all they were cracked up to be, and started walking back here."

"Here?"

"Yeah. Got as far as the pub on the outskirts of town, and you know the rest."

"So he was hiding in plain sight for two whole weeks?"

"Yep. Just shows you. Some people are invisible."

"Or easy to ignore."

I made a mental note. Even if Mike wasn't coming back to *The Hard Times*, I wanted his story about his two weeks on the street.

Trial by Social Media

While the police were seemingly satisfied with Mike's story and assumed his innocence beyond the whole absconding-from-prison lark, the tabloid press—led by Tinker—had other ideas.

The *Mail* dug up one of Mike's kidnap victims and went to town on just how evil the man was. Plenty of people took the bait, with a growing number of social media sleuths and so-called citizen journalists amplifying the narrative.

Tinker's venom was bad enough, but at least his "reporting" was still governed—loosely—by IPSO. The real trouble started when some blowhard right-wing pundit posted a 30-second YouTube clip, essentially calling for a public lynching. That was all it took for Cragsholme to fill up with complete randoms, armed with selfie sticks and completely unfounded opinions.

Andrea's face was everywhere on social media, which lurched from one wild theory to the next. She was dead. Mike had eaten her. Her baby had been stolen from her womb and sold to a grooming gang. Nothing was too ridiculous when it came to collecting clicks and likes.

Despite its remote location, people started flocking to the prison gates, demanding to be let in. As one of the most secure locations in the country, they didn't stand a chance. But when they started offering officers money for inside knowledge and flying drones over the walls, the shit really hit the fan.

HMP North Shore went into full lockdown, with a small army of armed police controlling the access roads.

Even though it was relatively easy to physically keep snoopers out of the jail, their voices still carried inside via the countless illicit smartphones that had been smuggled in.

Tony was particularly affected by all the commotion. He was still coming into work, but his mood was clearly subdued.

"I'm worried about him."

"I hear you, Sally, but what can we do?"

"I've asked Oliver to keep an eye on him, but they spend so much time locked behind those doors. Who knows what's going on in their heads?"

Bart Sellers' voice crackled over the radio.

"I've spoken to the Prime Minister, and he's agreed that, while we get to the bottom of this awful situation for my family, I take a step back from my responsibilities as a member of this government. At this time, I urge anyone who has any information about the whereabouts of my daughter, Andrea, to contact the police and not fuel the very upsetting gossip and innuendo on social media. Beyond that, I would like to ask the public and the press to respect the privacy of my family at this very difficult time. Thank you."

Journalists called out as he walked away.

"Do you believe Michael Peterson had nothing to do with your daughter's disappearance?"

"Do you have a message for Andrea?"

The office, which had been listening intently, fell silent—apart from the sound of a grown man sobbing.

Sally quietly walked over to Tony, put her arm around him, and led him toward the door.

"I'm just taking Tony for a cigarette."

For the longest time, nobody said a word.

Hounded by the Mob

With Filip taking firm control of the commercial side of the business, Apollo was adopting a more... "remote" approach to work.

"Are we still paying him?"

"He's the boss's son—what can I do?"

"What *does* he do?"

"Your guess is as good as mine."

With no access to the team inside the prison, Sally, Bev, and I had come under increasing scrutiny from a growingly aggressive crowd of social media influencers. They followed us everywhere, filming our every move. Apollo, however, seemed immune to it all. His lack of visibility made him a less obvious link to *The Hard Times*, and they left him alone.

I'd become used to people shouting at me in the street.

"Are you protecting Andrea's killer?"

Years of working in the media had taught me to say nothing. Anything I did say would have been twisted into complete fantasy. Despite this, my silence was viewed as guilt, fuelling all manner of bizarre assumptions.

Sally had it worse. Her sexuality was weaponised against her. You think you're living in an enlightened age—until you hear the words *filthy* and *disgusting* hurled at a friend's relationship. She held them in complete contempt, and I suspect she would have rather spat in their faces than dignify them with a response.

The only person who did engage with the baying social media mob was Gabe. As a taxi driver, it was in his nature to talk to passengers and—ever the cliché—share his often wild and frequently unfounded opinions. Overnight, he became quite the meme.

I'll be honest—I worried about what I told him and what he was sharing.

Unmasking Apollo

Apollo's anonymity wasn't going to last forever. It started with one short post that quickly went viral.

"Who is Apollo and what does he know about Andrea Sellers?"

The post featured a photo stolen from his Facebook page—Apollo on his gap year in Thailand, grinning in the sun, beer in hand.

As more people jumped into the theory, other images of Apollo posing with Andrea surfaced. At first, these were playful photos of a young couple in love.

"Could this rich kid have the answers we're all looking for?"

Then, more intimate photos appeared.

"Is Apollo the masked hunk on Andrea's OnlyFans account?"

The general consensus was yes.

Bev was apoplectic with rage.

"Why the fuck have they dragged my Apollo into this? That's *clearly* not him. He doesn't even have a tattoo!"

Sally poured fuel on the fire.

"I don't mean to be rude, Bev, but have you seen him in the bath lately?"

Bev shook uncontrollably, her finger jabbing into Sally's face.

"Give me *one more reason*, and I'll see you marched out of that fucking door faster than you can say—"

Suddenly, another voice cut through the conversation. A much calmer voice. The voice of someone who had been carefully considering their options for some time.

"Miss, there is something you should know."

It was Tony.

"I've been getting phone calls and text messages about Andrea."

"Really?"

"I think they're from Apollo."

Bev's face slowly turned towards Tony, then me. It was a whole new kind of ugly.

"Fucking ridiculous. Sally, is it half-past yet? Get these boys back to the wing. We'll have no more talk of this nonsense."

As soon as the boys were patted down and sent back to their wings, Bev made her excuses and left.

Sally looked at me.

"What do you think, Euan?"

I exhaled.

"I think we need to speak with the Governor. But first, we *need* to speak with Tony."

Whispers and Burner Phones

When the lads arrived back in the office for their afternoon shift, I invited Tony for a cigarette.

"I didn't know you smoked, sir."

"I don't. But with everything going on, I might just start. Look, Sally's given us half a packet. They're yours if you want them."

Tony took the packet and smiled.

"Cheers."

"So, what you said about Apollo this morning—was that legit?"

"For the record, I ain't no snitch, but that cunt's got it coming."

"We're going to have to see that phone."

"Sure. Why not?"

"This could get you in a lot of trouble."

"Sir, the woman I love is missing. Going without a few privileges for being a naughty boy doesn't worry me. Besides, those Mr Kipling cakes you keep bringing in are making me fat. I don't need any more chocolate."

"Good lad."

"When did you get the phone?"

"A couple of days after Mike went missing. I didn't even want it. But I was told to keep a hold of it for someone and monitor any messages."

"Who?"

"No idea. Just some young lad on the wing that gave it to me. Don't know who he was holding it for. You don't ask questions. I thought I was just taking messages for someone to earn a bit of pocket money."

"I understand."

"But it became apparent pretty quickly that those messages were for me. They wanted to know where I'd hidden my share of the haul."

"Go on."

"I kept telling them—there was no money. That's when they told me they had Andrea."

"And this was all by text?"

"Originally, yeah. Different number every time. Obviously burner phones."

"So what makes you think Apollo is involved?"

"It's when the calls started. They really started piling the pressure on. Said they were going to hurt Andrea. The guy had an accent like Mike. But, you know, without the stammer."

"OK."

"I thought it was one of his boys from his old gang in Bristol. But I kept hearing this posh voice whispering in the background, telling him what to say. Sounded a real pain in the arse."

"Well, that certainly sounds like Apollo. But we're going to need more evidence if we're going to the Governor with this."

"Well, it's just a gut feeling. But you're always telling us to trust our gut. The guy with the Bristol accent just knew too much about me. He told me things about conversations I've had at work—with Oliver or Mike."

"What sort of conversations?"

"You know, little scams, previous capers, and all that stuff."

"Previous capers? What, like where you hid your money from that last big job?"

"Jesus, sir! Don't *you* start. There *is* no money. No, I'm talking about other stuff, things I can only assume Apollo had overheard. The thing is, I know Mike wasn't there when I told Oli some of those things. And Oli ain't no snitch or gossip. I know I can trust him."

My next move depended on whether I could trust Tony or not.

I'd be a fool to trust a career criminal and everyday idiot like Tony.

But, call it journalist gut instinct—I *did* trust him.

Collateral Damage

"WHAT THE FUCK HAVE YOU DONE!"

"Hello, Bev. How are you?"

"NEVER FUCKING MIND HOW I AM. What have you done?"

"A colleague reported something—an allegation which I believed needed further investigation."

"THEY FUCKING KICKED HIS FRONT DOOR IN AND DRAGGED HIM AWAY AT GUNPOINT!"

"Apollo?"

"YES! FUCKING APOLLO. WHO DO YOU THINK I WAS TALKING ABOUT? MY SON. YOUR BOSSES' SODDING SON, APOLLO."

"I didn't really have a choice."

"There is always a choice. I've made a choice. Don't come in tomorrow. I will be acting editor until we get Lucy back from maternity leave. Is that clear?"

"If you are telling me I'm fired, I guess that's very clear."

"I am, and you are. I've spoken to the prison and requested that you are not granted access to the office again. Sally will collect your personal stuff and arrange a time to drop it off. We'll need your laptop back. You're already locked out of the system."

"Thank you."

What on Earth was I thanking her for? I walked into that office every day with nothing more than a Tupperware sandwich box full of sweet treats. I had no personal items to collect.

"And might I remind you, you signed a comprehensive NDA when you joined us. If I see anything in the papers connected to *The Hard Times*, my family, or this prison, my lawyers will fucking eat you alive. Understand?"

I really couldn't be arsed with the conversation anymore. I doubted I was getting paid for the time, so I terminated the call and texted Sally.

Leaving drinks tonight in Spoons. 7pm xxx

She replied instantly.

Best not. Bev is on the warpath. Maybe next week. Take care x.

A Hard Times Shaped Hole

All of a sudden, there was a big *Hard Times*-shaped hole in my life. It wasn't just the newspaper. It was the lads. Who'd have thought I could ever miss a bunch of violent thieves, drug dealers, and murderers?

I'd broken the cardinal rule of working with offenders—I'd become fond of them. I may even have thought of some of them as friends. But unlike any of my former colleagues from any other job, the chances of ever hearing from any of them again were highly unlikely and probably not recommended. I wouldn't find these guys on LinkedIn or Facebook, even if I wanted to. It was stupid, but I was mourning the loss of their friendship.

Not that the newspapers would let me forget them. Every day, there was an exposé about one of *The Hard Times* crew and some tenuous link to Andrea's disappearance.

As the love interest, father of the baby, and with the added bonus of an alleged hidden fortune, Tony was front-page news most days. God only knows how his anxiety was coping with all this.

Oliver also got his fair share of coverage—albeit more as a Page Seven fella. I had no doubt his mailbox would be filling up with letters from the kind of women who could look beyond a couple of convictions for murder in the hunt for a potential husband.

As for Mike, well, with his form, he was obviously hiding his guilt well.

Andrea continued to take up a lot of column inches, but the papers were more interested in the body she flaunted on OnlyFans than the smart, articulate young woman she was.

Hopefully, she was more than just a body at this stage of the story.

But the biggest story of the week was Apollo's arrest and subsequent release.

The papers wouldn't have touched this normally, but Apollo had approached them with his side of the story—a tale about a jealous love rival and a gullible boss taken in by the lies of a violent but charming man. It was tabloid gold.

My phone was ringing off the hook with offers of freelance work—spilling the beans on my former colleagues. But I also had Bev's threats of legal action if I breached my NDA and spoke to the press. It was unusual to be in such high demand while feeling so bloody useless at the same time. I'll be honest, it felt shit. I was lonely.

The phone rang, and I was about to ignore it when I saw Gabe's name on the caller ID.

"Gabe. How are you?"

"Not too bad, Euan. How are you, buddy?"

I thought Gabe might be sore after losing my trade. I was wrong.

"You wouldn't believe how busy I've been recently, running all those internet sleuths around town."

"Yeah. They won't leave me alone."

"Oh, they all want to know all about you. And Mike and Tony, of course. I don't tell them anything, of course. Well, unless they tip well—and some tip really well."

"Well, I don't grudge you anything, Gabe. You might as well make some hay while the sun shines. They'll be on to something else next week."

"Oh, I know that, but a little extra cash that the taxman won't see is always welcome. Hey, do you fancy a coffee? I guess you're too busy?"

"Not at all. I'd enjoy that."

"Cool, I'll pick you up in 30 minutes."

A Hot Flask of Coffee

Coffee to Gabe didn't mean a Starbucks or Costa. Gabe had a flask. I didn't mind. I appreciated the company as we parked up on the breakwater of Cragsholme docks.

"I like it here. It reminds me of when I was a kid and men had real jobs. Going out to sea. Those jobs were an adventure, not slowly dying of boredom behind the wheel of a taxi."

"So, tell me about some of the people you've been driving about recently."

"God. Some of them are proper nutters. What do they call themselves? Citizen journalists. They're not proper journalists like you."

"Just a selfie stick and a lot of front?"

"Yeah. One of them. Lovely girl. She had a lot of front. Do you know what I mean?"

"Are you talking about tits again, Gabe? What would Sharon say?"

Gabe blushed.

"Do you fancy coming along on a ride with one of them tomorrow?"

"What? One of your YouTubers?"

"Yeah. They're asking for you."

"I don't know, Gabe. I don't think that's a good idea."

"Maybe not. But I had to ask. She tips well."

"Well, in that case, you keep her sweet, but I'm going to have to say no."

"Well, would you mind if I gave her your telephone number?"

"Are you on a commission or something?"

"She just wants to speak to you. Can't do any harm, can it?"

"Oh, Jesus, Gabe. Is she hot?"

"Ha! Would that make a difference?"

"Listen, I've just spent the best part of a year locked up in a portacabin office with a bunch of hardened criminals, a butch lesbian, and Bev. Do you blame me for asking?"

"Sally isn't butch."

"Oh, go on then, Gabe. Give her my number, but no promises. She better not be weird."

Gabe dropped me off in town. Keen to top up on coffee that didn't come from a Thermos, I grabbed a copy of *The Guardian* and *The Sun* from the Co-op and settled into a quiet corner of Costa.

Both papers ran stories on Andrea's disappearance and the prison. *The Guardian*'s piece featured a report from a police press conference where Bart Sellers made an emotional plea for the safe return of his daughter. *The Sun* ran three pages of photos of Andrea in her underwear, a rogues' gallery featuring the news team of *The Hard Times* highlighting their crimes, and an opinion piece by Tinker, slating HMP North Shore as a pathetic excuse for a prison that prioritised inmates' feelings over punishment.

My phone rang. It was Gabe's YouTuber.

"I've been expecting your call. Maybe not so quickly, but still."

"Hiya, Euan. My name is Terri. Very big on YouTube. 2.5 million subscribers. You might know me. No? I'd love it if you'd come out for a ride around Cragsholme with me and Gabe tomorrow."

"Listen, Terri. That sounds great, but you must know I'm a professional journalist. I'm not really in the market to put myself out there on YouTube just yet."

"Oh no, darling. No. I wasn't thinking that. This is such a big story. I'm going multi-media and doing a proper grown-up podcast. 100% audio. I won't make you look silly on my old YouTube channel. I'm just after your insight, really."

"Really?"

"Yeah. My audience is growing up. They haven't got time for silly little YouTube videos anymore. They want to listen to something with a bit more meat on the bone. You know, when they're at the gym or out and about in the car. And you, Euan darling, are my first prime rack of ribs."

She made a sound like she was sucking her fingers playfully.

"This could be juicy. Are you in, Euan?"

I'm ashamed to say that I am not immune to being flirted with.

"Right. I'm under an NDA. I can't really talk about the paper."

She cut me short.

"But you can talk about the concept of prison, the men in there, how we treat them, prison reform, employment, training and education, how prisons are reflected in the media, and all that good stuff—right?"

"Wow! That does sound very grown up."

"Yeah. Well, I've always seen myself as more of a Stacey Dooley than a Zoella. You know, more hard-hitting stuff rather than the shopping hauls that everyone's doing—but still fun. That's the world I want to break into."

It was an interesting idea. Perhaps we could kill two birds with one stone.

"How about we do this? Let's meet up, have a bit of a chat, and see where it takes us."

I was thinking maybe I could pitch a feature to a few editors as a freelancer about what happens to influencers when they outgrow their audience. Also, I was keen to learn how these podcasts were put together. Every day is a school day. Although, in reality, I had nothing better to do.

Hard Times and Harder Choices

Sally was sitting waiting for me in Wetherspoons. She had already got the beers in.

"Good girl, Sally. It's nice in here, isn't it?"

Sally looked around at what was left of the day drinkers, some of whom were now putting in a considerable amount of overtime.

"Do you really think so?"

"No. It's fucking horrible. But it's lovely to see you, Sally. How've you been?"

"You see it all."

"And work? How are the lads?"

Sally sat back in her seat. "Well, we're missing Mike and Tony. He's on a charge for that phone, and I don't think he'll be coming back."

"He must be gutted?"

"The lads tell me he's fine. Apparently, he fancies a bit of a career change."

"Well, he was never going to be a journalist. What's he going to do?"

"Said he wants to get trained up to fix shoes and cut keys. Fancies himself working in one of those little huts outside Tesco."

"Maybe retail will suit him."

"He's always saying that he's a people person."

"Yeah. Tell that to the driver of that security wagon he tied up and left for dead. How's Bev doing?"

"Well, she's a fucking idiot. I don't think her heart is in it anymore. Back in the day, she was a force to be reckoned with. But now? Well, for a start, she's got no idea how the computers work and really has no intention of learning."

"So how's that going?"

"Ha! You're going to like this."

"I bet I don't."

"Apollo's back."

"Yeah. I heard they let him go. Couldn't pin anything on him. Shame."

"From what I understand, all the police got was 'no comment'. Like a broken record. They must go home with that phrase ringing in their ears, they hear it so much. Doesn't matter if you've got a free cop shop duty solicitor or a million-pound lawyer, that's all the advice they ever give out. So anyway, he's back at *The Hard Times*, and Bev has appointed him as the deputy editor."

"Fuck off!"

"Oh, but there is some good news. Filip is now properly, fully in charge of commercials. We might actually make some money this month—or at least until the advertisers see the state of the paper."

Sally pulled the latest copy of *The Hard Times* from her bag.

"When did we start using American English?"

"Ever since Apollo didn't know how to change the settings on his spellcheck. Oliver and Gary have tried to fill the void left by yourself and Mike. They're good, but they are more enthusiastic than forensic, like Mike was. We're really missing Mike. What about you? How are things going?"

I told Sally about my conversation with Terri.

"Ah, yes, Terri. We've had her on the phone, talking about her podcast. She really wanted to interview Oliver. He has that lovely Geordie accent, doesn't he? Of course, Bev killed the idea in the water. There was no way the Governor would let that happen. Now, what was it Terri called him?"

"A prime rack of ribs?"

"Ha! Where did you get that from? Nearly. A nice bit of T-bone, I think it was."

Great. My ego already felt like a burst sausage.

Breaking the Rules

That night, I brushed up on Terri's YouTube content. A good-looking Black girl. What was it with Gabe and good-looking Black girls? Perhaps she was his type. Sharon obviously didn't get the memo.

Her content was vapid at best. But it seemed to resonate with her audience. She wasn't lying about her 2.5 million followers, and the views on any one of her videos would have eclipsed the daily readers of any newspaper I had ever worked for.

Terri's presenting style was very loud—like a drama school brat, all tits and teeth—so I was very surprised when she rolled up the next morning in Gabe's cab looking much more subdued in jeans, a black sweater, and with cropped hair.

"Terri?"

"Euan. It's wonderful to finally meet you. Gabe has told me so much about you. Come and grab a seat here with me in the back."

"You look completely different from what I expected. I watched some of your videos last night."

"What did you think?"

"Well..."

I really didn't know what to say.

"Ha! I got you. Don't worry, you're not really in my target demographic. But that's about to change. By the way, what do you think of my new look? This is the new Terri."

"Um... Very nice."

Again, I was lost for words.

"Nice? NICE? That's not what any girl wants to hear when she asks you how she looks. Stunning works. Try stunning."

Gabe chuckled in the front seat.

"She's going to eat you alive, Euan. Didn't I tell you she was great?"

Knowing I was being played with, I changed the subject and got down to business.

"So, what do you want to do today?"

"Well, let's just get this mic on you and we'll have a little drive around and a bit of a chat."

"Do you have any prepared questions?"

"Nah. I prefer just to see where the conversation takes us. It's more organic. More authentic."

Gabe had put together a little itinerary, showcasing the best that Cragsholme had to offer. The road out to the prison as far as the police cordon. The beach. The docks. The high street, where we double-parked outside Boots to watch Mike's homeless friends cook up.

As we drove around, we just talked. Surprisingly, we talked about issues that seemed important. We talked about crime and punishment, rehabilitation, the promise of opportunity, and the reality of the situation for many of the men who found themselves behind the walls of HMP North Shore. Gabe was unusually quiet but appeared to be listening intently.

Terri led the conversation and, to be honest, was just brilliant. She had the enviable talent of being able to speak with incredible eloquence and confidence. But she also possessed a common touch. She had an East End London accent that gave her an edge but was a long way from the gutter. I was at a loss to understand why she had not been snapped up by a mainstream media company.

"I'm doing about ten grand a month on YouTube. Maybe as high as twenty if I get lucky and something goes viral. I don't know many people in traditional media earning that much—unless, of course, you're looking at the top dogs, but they are few and far between. Plus, I get all the freedom to do what I want. Why would I work for anyone else?"

She had a point. Terri could earn more in a couple of months than I would in a year in a job like *The Hard Times*. Not that I had to worry about that anymore.

"You stick with me, Euan lad. I'll show you how it's done."

I didn't doubt her for a second.

"So how did you get into this? Did you study media at college or something?"

"Ha! Absolutely not. I started filming myself on my smartphone when I was about 17. Just started talking about whatever caught my attention. Fashion, music, make-up, celebrities—I did it all."

"So what made you stand out from the crowd?"

"Absolutely nothing. The thing is, nobody saw my first hundred or so videos, but I learned a lot and developed my own style. I found my audience around about the same time I found myself. You could say I was an overnight success. It only took me five years."

"So what kept you going when nobody was watching?"

"I was pigheaded. Wouldn't listen to anyone. To be honest, I think I might be on the spectrum. You know, ADHD. I have so many ideas. The thing is, most people with ADHD have too many ideas and don't finish anything before jumping onto the next project. I'm a completionist. I get things done. If you want to be successful, you've got to finish things."

"So, you don't actually have a diagnosis for ADHD?"

"Nah. Why would I need to see a doctor about that when I have Google on my phone?"

I couldn't help but think Terri had a lot in common with some of the guys I'd met in HMP North Shore. Like them, she broke the rules. The only difference was that she picked up a smartphone instead of a drug habit, a knife, or a gun.

I also thought we shared a lot of commonality. I too had many grand ideas—most of them abandoned in the wake of a shambolic life. It was only the strict deadlines imposed by working for a newspaper that kept me on track. Perhaps Terri could teach me a thing or two.

A Chase With Terri Talks

The podcast sounded amazing. Terri played it to me over coffee. We sat in Costa's window like a pair of teenagers, sharing a single set of earphones.

"You like it?"

"I fucking love it. You've made me sound like I know what I'm talking about."

Like most people, I've never liked the sound of my own voice. As such, I had never really considered making the move from print to broadcast media as so many other former colleagues had done. Perhaps there was a future in this podcasting lark and maybe even the promise of resurrecting my journalistic career after the abrupt ending of my job at *The Hard Times*.

"How did you make it sound so good?"

"Decent mics and good editing software."

"I didn't even hear a single 'um' or 'err'."

"Doh! That's because I spent five hours editing them out last night. But I'm glad you like it."

Terri pulled her phone out and started tapping and swiping on the screen.

"So when's it going live?"

"Now! It's live for the world to hear. Pull your chair around. I need to get you on camera."

Before I could protest, she had us both in shot and started live streaming.

"Hello, hello, hello. It's your girl Terri here."

Her volume had increased by a good 10%.

"I'm here in Cragsholme grabbing a coffee with my new best friend, Euan. Ain't he lovely?"

She hugged me theatrically. I think I may have recoiled in shock. The last person to cuddle me was Tony after I had provided a soundboard to a particularly emotional tale of childhood trauma.

"Euan's given me the lowdown on what life is really like behind those cold prison walls at HMP North Shore. Seriously, this guy has spent the best part of a year with some of the most dangerous men in the country, and I think—no, strike that—I *know* he understands what makes them tick better than anyone else. This brave, smart man has broken bread with people who, just a few years ago, would have eaten your face. We're talking proper *Silence of the Lambs* stuff here. This guy is a lion tamer. But these lions are men. Men who have killed and much worse."

I interrupted. "I really don't think we can say that."

"And there he is. Humble to the very end."

I could see on her phone's screen that there were already a couple of thousand people on the stream. Little red hearts floated up over the video, showing her followers' appreciation.

"Yesterday, we talked and talked. That's right, girls, I think we've got chemistry. What do you think, Euan?"

She didn't give me time to answer.

"I just *know* you'll want to hear more, and so I'm incredibly excited to announce the launch of my new podcast, *Terri Talks*. It's available now wherever you get your podcasts, but don't forget—subscribers to my Patreon will have access to an absolute *ton* of bonus content and gossip. And if you like what you hear, please like and share. Tell your friends, tell your mother, tell your brother, tell your sister, and tell your lover—because Terri *loves* to talk. Laters, haters."

Everyone in the coffee shop was staring at us. Terri had absolutely no fear or sense of embarrassment about performing in public. Some people looked on in annoyance. Others were bemused or even laughing. She really didn't care what people thought of her. Maybe she was right about being on the spectrum after all.

Her focus suddenly changed.

"Who's that?"

Terri pointed at a man through the window, purposely walking on the other side of the street.

"Fuck me. That's Apollo."

Apollo was walking down the street with what looked like two bags of groceries.

"He's been to Iceland. Funny, I always assumed Bev was more of a Waitrose shopper."

"Come on. Let's follow him."

We ran out onto the street and followed him from a safe distance. Terri held onto my arm, giggling with excitement. She was having *way* too much fun for what was essentially a stroll down Cragsholme High Street.

Our pursuit didn't last long. Apollo looked like he was heading to the train station.

"Perhaps he's heading down to London. He's always banging on about some uni mate who works in the city. You know, projecting his friend's success to conceal his own failure."

But on arrival at the station, he jumped into a taxi.

"Shit. We've lost him."

"Not quite. Did you see who his driver was?"

"Gabe?"

"Brilliant."

"Sorry, silly question."

"Go on."

"Why did you want to follow him?"

"Let's just say I had a funny feeling in my stomach."

Trusting Your Gut

Gabe was back on the rank within twenty minutes.

"Where did you take him?"

"Who?"

"Apollo."

"Oh, that lanky streak of piss. Bloody mummy's boy."

"The very same. Where'd he go?"

"Well, that's the funny thing. Asked me to take him to that horrible little shopping precinct on the Beaches Estate."

"Where?"

"The Beaches Estate. How long have you lived in Cragsholme? It's notorious. I refuse to go there after dark. It's bloody horrible. Full of junkies. What the fuck Apollo is doing there is beyond me. Must have a woman on the go. Or a bloody habit."

"Can you take us there?"

"Well, seeing as I like your cash almost as much as I like your company, jump in."

Gabe wasn't exaggerating. Even by Cragsholme's incredibly low standards, the Beaches Estate was a complete shithole.

"It wasn't always like this. I had mates living on this estate when I was growing up."

Gabe pointed to the top-floor flat of a three-storey building, half the windows boarded up.

"That's where my buddy Jimmy lived. Scottish lad. Family came down to work in the fishing industry. Everyone worked in the fishing industry in those days. Either on the boats, on the docks, or packing fish in the factories. Wasn't for me. Fucking stinks, but the money was good. Nobody got rich, apart from the boat owners, but they had dignity. Mind you, the only thing Jimmy ever caught was hepatitis from a dirty needle. When the fishing ended, this place lost its way, and I'm sad to say so did Jimmy."

"Do you ever see him?"

"Not since he died. Must be twenty-odd years ago now. Before then, he spent a few years in your old place."

"North Shore?"

"Yeah. His mum always said he never looked better than when he was in that prison. Three square meals and a chance to stay clean."

"Gabe, honey. We really need to get you on a podcast. You have so many stories."

"But none with a happy ending. Talk about Grimms' tales."

We drove past a flat-roofed pub with a dust bowl of a beer garden. A broken glass sat underneath the rusty frame of a children's swing. Gabe slowed down and pointed towards a row of flats above some largely boarded-up shops.

"That's it. That's where I dropped him off."

It looked like a crack den.

"Keep driving. We don't want him to see us."

"What the fuck is Apollo doing there?"

Gabe's phone rang.

"Shit! It's him."

"Answer it."

Gabe answered on speakerphone.

"Hi, Dave. Apollo. Can you pick me up in twenty and drop me off at my mother's?"

Gabe looked at me in his rear-view mirror. I nodded.

"Sure thing! I'll give you a beep when I'm outside."

"Dave?"

"He always calls me that, the ignorant sod. I've stopped trying to correct him."

"Listen, why don't you drop us off at that pub, hang around for ten minutes, and then go pick him up?"

"I can do that. But are you sure you want to go there? I'm not sure it's a place I'd take a woman."

"Hey! Look here, 'Dave', I'm tougher than I look. Maybe it's Euan here that needs taking care of."

She wasn't wrong.

Gabe had nothing to worry about. The Beaches Inn, as we discovered the pub was called, was empty apart from an old boy nursing a half-decent-looking pint of Guinness.

It was a huge room with a little dance floor and lights in the corner. The rest of the venue had the most disgusting brown and red, heavily stained, cigarette-burned carpet.

"Jesus. When did they ban smoking in pubs? This place still stinks."

Terri nodded over to the old man in the corner. He was fumbling with a lighter.

"I don't think smoking was ever banned in here. The independent state of The Beaches."

"It's like that pub, The Jockey, in *Shameless*."

"*Shameless*?"

"Yeah. TV show. Channel 4, I think. Maybe I'm showing my age."

"Don't worry. I love a silver fox."

She was definitely playing with me. To my shame, I was letting her.

The barmaid looked like she had a story to tell. As wide as she was tall, I wouldn't bet against her in a fight against Bev. She didn't just look like she had balls. She looked like she might collect the balls of her unfortunate victims in a jar behind the bar.

"A pint of Stella and… what wines do you have?"

She looked at me as if I was crazy. Terri interrupted.

"Two pints of Stella, please."

"Sit down, love. I'll bring them over."

We walked over to a little table by the window, overlooking the car park.

"She's like a Rottweiler. Fierce-looking but friendly enough."

"I dare you to try and tickle her belly."

"She'd have my hand off."

The barmaid came over with the drinks.

"Mind if I join you?"

"Sure."

I gestured to an empty seat, and she sat down.

"I'm Violet. Although they call me Daisy around here."

"I love the flower names. If I had a girl, I'd call her Rose."

"No, nothing to do with that. It's because I'm the size of a fucking cow."

She let out a huge laugh and slapped me on my back with a force that knocked the wind out of me. She turned to Terri.

"I know you, don't I?"

"I don't know. Do you?"

"YouTube. My daughter's a big fan. She'll be totally stoked to hear you've been in here. Which brings up the question…"

"Go on?"

"What the fuck are you doing in here?"

We all laughed. Perhaps we'd found a friend in the most unfriendly-looking of places. Never judge a book by its cover.

On the way back into town, we drove past the flat Apollo had been visiting. The lights were on, and we could see people moving about.

"Stop the car, Gabe. I'm going to knock on the door. Terri, stay here."

As I walked up to the door and pressed the intercom, I really didn't know what I was going to say. Too late.

"Hello."

"Hello. I'm looking for Dave."

"Who?"

"Dave. Is he in?"

"Kate, do you know anyone called Dave? No one here called Dave."

The flat window opened, and a young man stuck his head out.

"Is that you, Euan? It fucking is! How you doing? Great to see you."

It was Billy, our former graphic designer and unofficial prison tattooist.

"I got out last week. Come on up. Bev's just sent us some food up. We're having pizza."

I declined the offer but continued the conversation from the street.

It turned out the Bev might actually have a heart of gold after all..

Bev had apparently bumped into Billy on Cragsholme High Street and was worried that he wasn't coping. Billy never looked particularly well-fed, but on this occasion, he appeared thoroughly malnourished. His clothes hung off him, his skin was pale, and there was a gauntness to his face that suggested he hadn't eaten properly in days.

Bev gave him the details of a local charity that could provide support through the food bank. But she didn't stop there. She promised to send Apollo around to his flat with a week's worth of shopping.

It turned out Apollo was just running errands for his mum. Soft lad. You can't always trust your gut.

Doing Time

The next few days were quiet. Terri had gone back down to London, and with no new leads, the news cycle had largely moved on from Andrea's disappearance.

I had a lot of time on my hands. I even bought a microphone and started playing around with the idea of a podcast. I thought I could do something on prison reform and rehabilitation, but without access to a fully functioning prison, I was struggling. Everything I recorded sounded shit. Sally kept me in the loop regarding the everyday office dramas at *The Hard Times*.

"Filip's had some good news. His release date has been moved forward, and just as soon as all the paperwork is done, he'll be sent back to Poland in the next two weeks or so."

"Well, that is good news."

"Good news for Filip, but bad news for the rest of us. The paper will be bankrupt within the year unless we find a new Filip."

"Or a new Andrea."

There was a brief awkward silence that required immediate small talk to fill.

"What about the other lads? How are they doing?"

"Harry sends his regards."

"How's he doing?"

"To be honest, he's looking tired. He misses you. It was his birthday last week—64. He'd probably be thinking about retirement if he were on the outside."

"Is that even an option inside?"

"Well, kind of. The system doesn't insist on offenders working beyond retirement age. But what else are they going to do?"

"Sit on their bed and quietly go crazy watching some idiot mopping the wing. What a way to grow old."

"Well, most don't have that problem."

"What do you mean?"

"How else do you want me to put it? They die young."

"Really?"

"Yeah. We ran a story about it in the paper last year. Maybe just before you started. There was some medical journal—The BMJ, I think it was. They said the average life expectancy of a prisoner in the UK was 67, or something like that."

"Compared to what?"

"Oh, I don't know. 86 or 87."

"Is it really? Fuck, it's cruel, isn't it? The system locks you up for the best years of your life and then robs you of 20 years on top of that."

I was making a mental note to pitch that idea to *The Guardian*.

"It gets worse. Guess how long prison officers live for?"

"Well, taking into account that most of them are chronic alcoholics and generally miserable bastards—no, I've no idea."

"59."

"Fuck. How old are you, Sally?"

"58."

"Well, it's been nice knowing you. How old is Bev?"

"I don't know. 104 maybe."

"At least."

"To be honest, she's looking pretty tired herself."

"Bev? She'll outlive the lot of us."

"Oh, I don't know. I reckon she'd walk away from it all if someone gave her the right offer."

"How much have you got in the bank, Sally?"

"Not enough to throw away on a rag like *The Hard Times*."

"I wouldn't even pay the £1.50 cover price with Apollo editing it."

"Why don't you call Bev?"

"Do you really think that would be a good idea?"

"It couldn't hurt."

Back Behind Bars

I was surprised to find myself back in HMP North Shore the following Monday, warmly greeted by Bev.

"First things first, Euan. We don't focus on the past here at *The Hard Times*. I think we both said things we might now regret. It's time to move on."

"Wow. I appreciate that. Thank you, Bev."

"The lads are all really excited to see you again. To be honest, the place has been a mess these past few weeks. I'm embarrassed by the quality of the papers we've put out. They've not been good enough, and it's up to you to get them back in shape."

"OK."

"We've lost some good people recently, and we're about to lose another one."

"Filip?"

"Yeah. We'll talk about him later. Listen, and this is hard for me to say as his mother, but Apollo wasn't really up to the job. We've let him go. That doesn't mean I forgive you for the ridiculous accusations you and that man Tony made about him. He's a good lad. I won't have his name dragged through the mud again."

"Understood."

"You should also know that I received an email from Lucy. She won't be coming back after maternity leave. Her husband has persuaded her that *The Hard Times* isn't a place for a young mum to work. Says it's too risky. Anyway, the full-time role as editor is yours to lose."

"Wow. Thank you."

"Don't let me down again."

With Bev's pep talk out of the way, it was time to assess the damage.

The lads had learned the previous week that Apollo was moving on. They'd been fed some cock-and-bull story about him taking up an opportunity more closely related to his degree. Nobody believed it. But once they heard I was coming back, they decided it wouldn't be fair for me to inherit the work ethic they'd adopted under Apollo's guidance.

The pagination for this week's issue, dictated by the volume of ads, had already been decided. The pages were prepped in Adobe InDesign, and non-time-sensitive content was waiting to be edited. I asked Harry to start tidying up the features pages while Oliver and I looked at the week's news agenda. I didn't even need to worry about the sports section. Despite muttering something about badminton being gay, Adam had it covered.

It was good to be back in the driving seat, feeling productive again. It was going to be a busy week, and we needed to find the time to recruit new guys to fill Mike and Tony's roles. But as a team, we pulled together.

"What are we going to do about Filip?"

"Not much we can do. He's booked on a flight back to Warsaw on Thursday. From the moment they open his cell that day, his feet won't touch the ground. He'll be back home in Poland before we put the paper to bed on Friday."

"Does he need to be here?"

"What do you mean?"

"Well, he's been doing the job from inside a maximum-security prison for months. Can't get much more remote than that. No reason why he can't do it from a different time zone."

"Are you listening to this, Filip?"

"I heard."

"And what do you think?"

"Is a good idea. I need a job. You need revenue. And I've still got a lot to learn before I start my own publication."

"Great. Sally, get Filip's address in Poland. Make sure he has a laptop and a mobile phone waiting for him when he arrives. We'll sort everything else out when you're on the ground. Might have to set up a little business in Poland. I'll get my lawyer onto it, get some advice."

"Perfect."

I loved this new approach to work. I think Terri would call it agile. It certainly felt agile.

Standing on the Edge of a Void

I met Tony on the other side of the closed gate. He was waiting to be let across the yard and into his new training centre. He looked manic.

"Sir! How are you, sir? I heard you were back. What the fuck are you doing here?"

"Well, I'm all the better for seeing you, Tony. How's the new job going?"

"It's good. I'm learning a lot. Turns out I'm pretty good with my hands."

"No more phone calls?"

"No. I decided I'm better off going incommunicado."

"Like the song."

"What?"

"'Incommunicado'—it's a song by… Oh, never mind. I'm probably showing my age. Big word. You swallowed a dictionary?"

"Hanging out with smart cunts like you, sir. No offence."

"Ha. None taken."

"Have you seen Mike?"

"T-t-that c-c-cunt? No, he's still over in the mad house with Gary. To be honest, glad to see the back of him. Always asking about that cash."

"The cash you haven't got?"

"Exactly."

"And how have you been otherwise?"

"Well, obviously I'm worried about Andrea and the baby, but the docs have put me on these new tablets and I can't stop smiling."

"And how's that going?"

"Fucking terrifying, really. It's like I'm happily standing on the edge of a void, totally oblivious to what's beyond. But to be honest, I'm more worried he'll take me off them. God knows how I'd feel without them."

"Well, Tony, it's good to see you smiling, but I've got to get off. We've got a newspaper to get out."

"And I've got shoes to fix and keys to cut. Do you think I could cut one to open that gate?"

"Don't even joke about it, Tony. You'll be back in solitary before you can say—"

"It wasn't me."

"That's right. Hey, do you fancy writing a review of your new job? Be good to feature some other opportunities in the paper."

"Nah. Bigger, better things to do in my pad at night. And besides, you're not the boss of me anymore."

Tony walked away from the gate with a fixed grin on his face. I wasn't sure if he was playing with me, or if it was the drugs.

A Familiar Face

Terri called the office.

"Hey, I'm back in town. Seeing as it's Friday night, fancy taking a girl out for a drink?"

"Sure thing. When and where?"

"6 p.m., straight after work, at The Beaches Inn."

"Are you kidding me?"

"No. I liked it there. Plus, I promised Daisy I'd swing by. Her daughter's going to be there."

Oliver was standing behind me, his hand on my shoulder.

"Sounds like you're on a promise there, sir."

"I doubt it, Oliver. I'm sure she'd much rather a bit of prime T-bone steak than these fatty ribs. I know what the friend zone looks like."

"So what made you want to come back to Cragsholme?" I asked.

"Well, you don't find such—how shall we call it—authentic local boozers like The Beaches down there in that London."

"The blokes aren't too bad either, are they?"

"Stop fishing, Euan."

I feigned disappointment, hoping I didn't show my real disappointment.

Daisy came bounding over, her mini-me in close pursuit—a ten-year-old ball of energy with a tangle of orange hair.

"OMG. Is it really you, Terri? Tiff will be so jealous when she hears about this. Can I have a photo for Insta?"

"Of course. What's your name?"

"Rachel. But you can call me Red."

I jumped into the conversation. "Because of the red hair? That's cool."

She looked at me as if I was a moron. "Who's that? Your dad? He's not the sharpest tool in the box, is he? Get out of my photo. There's no filter that would sort your face out."

Terri let out a laugh that would put Daisy to shame.

The pub door swung open, and in strolled a very familiar face. He walked straight up to the bar, ordered and sank a double vodka, then walked straight back out again.

"Fuck me. Do you know who that was?"

Terri looked at me blankly.

"That's Tinker. He looked distracted—worried, even. Can't believe he didn't see us."

"Tinker? The journalist? Really? Let's see where he's heading."

Chasing people down the street was becoming a bit of a habit when Terri was in town. She grabbed my hand and pulled me out of the pub.

"He's heading towards the precinct. Surely he doesn't know Billy."

"No, he's walking past."

Tinker walked to the end of the street and onto the next before casually looking over his shoulder and knocking on a door.

Terri urged me to stay back. "He knows who you are. He won't be suspicious if he sees me."

"What? 2.5 million YouTube followers. You're bloody famous."

"You're forgetting my makeover. Unless he's a fan, I doubt he knows me from Daisy back there."

The door opened just as Terri caught up with him. She had time for a quick glance before picking up the pace and making out she was running for a passing bus—which she accidentally caught and disappeared down the road.

My phone rang.

"Terri. What the fuck? Where are you going?"

"Hang on. I'm getting off at the next stop. You won't fucking believe this."

"What did you see?"

"Not what. Who. I'll see you back at the pub."

So Pretty

"Are you sure it was Andrea?"

"I'd swear on my grandmother's grave."

"What? Just standing there in the doorway letting Tinker in?"

"Yep."

"How did she look?"

"Great. She's so pretty."

I got up to leave.

"Where are you going?"

I lowered my voice. "Well, I'm damn sure that I ain't going to phone the police in this dodgy little pub. I'll do it from the car park."

What happened over the next sixty minutes was nothing short of impressive.

I'd never seen so many police vehicles amassed in the surrounding streets, all hidden out of view from the house concealing Tinker and his apparent hostage. Several drones were in the sky, and a helicopter circled the estate. I didn't imagine that was unusual for a Friday night.

There wasn't time to seal off the streets, so quite a crowd had formed around the scene. This was going to be played out under the glare of many smartphones. Ever the professional, she joined the ranks of amateurs all hoping for subscriptions, likes, and shares. Red was at the front of the crowd, taking her first steps towards becoming a micro-influencer.

Suddenly, as if someone had blown a whistle, a small army of armed response officers ran towards the house. They smashed their way in with a battering ram and, within a matter of seconds, bundled its occupants out into the street.

First Tinker, then Andrea, and then someone else. I couldn't believe my eyes. Or maybe I could.

"It's fucking Apollo."

Andrea was led calmly away by a female officer while Tinker and Apollo were cuffed and bundled into the back of two separate vans.

"ANDREA! Are you OK?"

She looked up at me and shook her head.

"What about the baby, Andrea? Is the baby OK?"

There was no answer.

"I'm going to have to call Bev. She's not going to like this."

Bev didn't pick up.

I turned towards Terri, but she was in full live broadcast mode.

"This is Terri Talks, live from the Beaches Estate in Cragsholme, where we have breaking news regarding the disappearance of Andrea Sellers, daughter of local MP Bart Sellers. Armed police have just rescued Andrea from a property on the estate, and two men have been taken into custody."

I'd had my suspicions for a long time, but I learned at this point that the newspaper industry was officially dead.

Live from The Beaches

With the police securing the crime scene, we retreated back to The Beaches.

The television screens, normally reserved exclusively for football, were all tuned to Sky News, which was running a constant rotation of smartphone footage from the estate. The regulars cheered every time a familiar face appeared on the screen.

Rachel screamed with excitement.

"They're using my video!"

Terri hugged her.

"How clever of you to send them your footage."

"I learned from the best."

Daisy was as proud as punch.

"My little girl Red, the big social media influencer. Giving you a run for your money, Terri."

Not that Terri had anything to worry about—her phone was ringing off the hook, with seemingly every TV and radio news show booking her for various slots.

"I've added 5,000 subscribers in the last hour. This is so fucking good."

I was constantly checking my emails, keen to highlight that I was also a very important journalist. Nobody was biting.

Local news crews had started amassing in the car park.

"I might nip out there in a minute and see if they need any help."

Terri patted my hand and gave me a reassuring smile.

"That's a good idea, dear."

Bart Sellers appeared on the TV screen. He was flanked by a senior-looking female police officer and someone who could have been the family lawyer or maybe a PR handler.

"Turn it up, Daisy."

"On behalf of my wife and myself, and of course our darling daughter Andrea, we would like to thank the police and members of the general public for all their assistance in bringing this unfortunate event to an end."

"Bloody hell. He's like a robot. Can he not show any emotion?"

"He's a politician. They are made that way."

Journalists shouted out.

"Mr Sellers, how is Andrea?"

The lawyer/PR handler spoke.

"Ms Sellers is currently getting checked over by doctors at Cragsholme Community Hospital. I'm sure you'd all like to wish her well, and of course, the family would like to thank everyone for their support. But we would also like to request that you respect the family's privacy at this time while they come to terms with these events."

"And her child? How is the baby?"

"No more questions. Thank you."

The spokesperson put an arm around Bart and turned him towards the house.

The police officer spoke.

"Please remember, this is now an ongoing criminal case. We know there's a lot of interest in this case, but we would urge everyone not to post anything on social media that could prejudice a trial."

Bart was led back into the family home. Just before he reached the front door, someone shouted something I think a lot of us were thinking.

"Is Andrea really pregnant? She doesn't look pregnant."

Bart turned around and appeared shocked but was quickly bundled into his home before anything else could be said.

Daisy came over.

"It's fucking crazy out there tonight. Seems like a good excuse for a lock-in. You want to stay?"

"What? With all the police outside? Isn't that asking for trouble?"

"Listen, love, after their shift ends tonight, they'll all be wanting a drink. A few out-of-hours beers isn't going to bother any of them. We've got a room upstairs if you two want to crash."

I looked over at Terri hopefully. She smiled. Then laughed.

"No thanks, love. I'm in the Holiday Inn Express, and Euan really needs to go home and get his beauty sleep."

"I'll phone Gabe."

The Rumour Mill

The mainstream media largely played by the rules. The next day's papers and news broadcasts all reported that two men, Tinker and Apollo, had been arrested in connection with the disappearance of Ms Sellers. But that was pretty much it. They'd now keep quiet about the case until proceedings started in court.

Social media, on the other hand, paid no attention to the rules. Every conceivable theory was being thrown around to feed the algorithm. Andrea's pregnancy was the biggest talking point. Was she or wasn't she?

I called Terri.

"How was your hotel?"

"I do love a Holiday Inn breakfast."

I looked at the burnt toast I was struggling to eat.

"Are you seeing all this shit on social media?"

"It's everywhere. Impossible to avoid."

"You're not getting involved in it, are you?"

"No. I know the rules, and honestly, I don't need the drama. Lots of people are tagging me into the conversation, though. So it's sending traffic my way without me even creating content. Have you spoken to Bev yet?"

"No. I've given up trying. I'll hopefully see her on Monday when I'm back at North Shore."

The next couple of minutes were just small talk. To be honest, Terri sounded distracted and uninterested. I could hear her typing away on a laptop as we spoke. Suddenly, she became more animated again.

"Shit! Have you seen what the BBC have just tweeted?"

"No?"

"A third person has been arrested in relation to the disappearance of Andrea Sellers."

She was quoting the post.

"Fuck me. Who is it?"

"I'm clicking on the link."

"Go on, go on."

"Who do you think it is?"

I knew straight away.

"Andrea?"

"Bingo!"

A Mother's Grief

Bev wasn't the kind of woman to show her emotions, but when she called me on Sunday night, I could tell she was trying to hold back the tears.

"I'm sorry I've not returned your calls, Euan. It's been a very difficult couple of…"

"I understand."

"Listen. I won't be in tomorrow, or probably any time this week…"

"That's OK."

"You and Sally have got everything under control. I trust you. I'll still be around online, helping Filip get set up now he's back over there. But you won't see me in the office. I doubt they'd let me in. They certainly wouldn't give me a key. If you want to get hold of me, probably best out of hours and not on the Hard Times email server."

"Understood."

Silence.

"How are you, Bev? Are you OK?"

"How am I?"

There was an extended pause. I heard Bev take several breaths, and then the floodgates opened.

"The stupid, stupid little boy. I was always too soft on him. Girls have always been able to take advantage of him. They can wrap him around their little fingers."

Another pause. I knew not to speak.

"Apollo isn't a criminal. He's not like the boys in North Shore. He's led a privileged life. We've given him everything. But he was snared by that stupid girl with her stupid ideas. His only crime was that he was in love."

"Andrea?"

"Don't mention that bitch's name. I rue the day I introduced that witch to him. She's ruined his life. We saw her and her family and thought, what a nice girl. Perfect for a boy like Apollo. She'd help him settle down, grow up a bit, maybe get a job with her father. It was perfect. But no. She didn't want that life. Behind the facade of the world she moved in, she was fucking feral. I mean, that filth on the internet. That's not Apollo."

Bev took another breath before continuing her manic episode.

"They were on one minute, then off the next. Apollo told me they had an open relationship and I was just too old-fashioned to understand. But I didn't understand. He's a handsome boy. Of course, it was all her idea. The fact is, he couldn't bear to be without her. Even if that meant she was fucking someone else."

"He must have been devastated when he heard about Tony."

"Oh, I suspect he knew all about Tony before anything happened. Just another one of her stupid fantasies that she tortured him with."

"So, have you spoken to him?"

"No. But I've spoken to his solicitor. What a fucking mess."

"So what's happening now?"

"Well, they've all been charged. All three of them. With God knows what. How can you kidnap yourself? They'll be up in front of the magistrates tomorrow and then on to the high court. No idea when that will happen. I'm not expecting any of them to get bail."

I remembered Andrea's little fantasy about being locked up. Careful what you wish for. Sadly for her, it wouldn't be in the company of men like Tony.

"Listen, Euan. I really appreciate you taking the time to listen to an old lady's troubles. I don't really have anyone else. I know we've had problems in the past, and I haven't always been kind. I don't tell you this enough—I really do respect you."

"Thank you, Bev."

I laughed. "But I don't think you've ever told me that."

"Oh, fuck off, you needy bastard."

She hung up.

"Goodnight then, Bev."

Monday Morning Banter

The guys were hyper as they filed into the office on Monday morning. I tried, largely in vain, to keep a lid on all the excitement.

"Good weekend, Sir? Anything happen?"

"No. Pretty quiet one, really. What about you, Oliver?"

"You know. We had a huge fucking party on the wing. It was awesome. Loads of birds and booze and pills. You know how we roll in this place."

"What he means is, he had a tin of tuna, a quiet wank, and a little cry in his pad."

"Yeah. Thanks for that, Harry. I really didn't need that image in my head this morning."

"Talking about birds. Who was that girl we saw you with on the news on Friday night?"

"That would be Terri. We're just good friends."

"Nah. Not the tidy black girl. She's well out of your league. That unit of a woman with the fat kid."

"What? Daisy? No."

"Ha ha. Daisy. Moooo!"

It took a while to settle the lads down, but they soon got into their work.

Oliver was working on a story about the possibility of telephones being installed in cells. Gary had an article almost ready to go on encouraging safer drug use in prisons. Harry was busy writing about a new theatre project designed to help young offenders develop their confidence. Apparently, Tony had signed up and was auditioning for a lead role. Judging by the smile on his face, he was loving every minute.

"What the fuck is Reiki? I'm not writing about this shit!"

"Come on, Adam. Play the game."

"There's only one fucking game I'm interested in. COME ON YOU FUCKING MILLWALL!"

A paper cup hit him squarely on the back of the head.

Just as I thought it was all about to kick off, Sally stood up and restored order with a cough.

"Good one, Oliver. You got me good."

Today would be a good day. The guys were in a great mood, the banter was flowing, and the work was getting done.

After lunch, I caught up with Gary.

"How's Mike doing? Is he still on your wing?"

"No, he's moved on. B Wing, I think. He's working in the library. Seems to like it there."

"That's good. Probably for the best he's moved on. I reckon you're going to get a couple of new guys on the induction wing tonight, and I don't reckon Mike would be too pleased to see them."

The Long Game

Gary kept us all entertained and informed with the latest from the induction wing over several extended smoke breaks.

"Apollo came onto the wing last night. He was alone. I think they've sent Tinker straight to the VP wing because, you know, he used to be a screw."

"And how was he?"

"He was clinging to the screws for dear life until he saw me. I told him that was a strategy likely to get him a beating. Now the stupid cunt won't leave me alone. He's so fucking freaked out. Won't shut up."

"So, what's he told you?"

"There's so much to unpack. I really don't know where to start."

"How about the beginning?"

The beginning actually started much earlier than any of us could have possibly believed.

Andrea, like many of the lads in the office, had become enthralled by the story of Tony's hidden stash. The more the lads teased Tony, the more convinced Andrea became that the money was real.

Tinker had simply poured fuel on the fire. He had been trying to doorstep her father about a story when Andrea caught his attention.

"I think old Bart deployed her to distract Tinker from a piece he was writing about an alleged affair with some parliamentary assistant. These guys will sell their own fucking daughters down the river to protect themselves. I'm not sure if she fucked him—Apollo didn't want to talk about that. But they got chatting about life in North Shore, and eventually, the conversation turned to Tony and his missing cash. They were both convinced it was real. Andrea made a deal: leave my dad alone, and I'll give you half the cash."

She'd seen how Tony—and half the other lads—looked at her, so she cooked up a plan. She'd flirt with them all, but she'd make Tony fall in love with her.

"Poor Tony didn't stand a chance. It was Andrea who persuaded him to encourage the lads to throw a little riot so he could get his leg over."

The pregnancy was faked—just another way to sink her hooks deeper into Tony. When her father and Bev decided to pack her off to Spain, she knew she had to move fast but wasn't sure what to do next.

"Tony must be devastated."

Oliver pitched in. "Fucking hard to tell these days. The stupid cunt walks around with that glazed grin on his face. He's dead behind the eyes, mate. Fuck knows what's going on in his head."

Mike going for a walkabout was a gift.

"An escaped prisoner who, like most of us, had clearly fallen under Andrea's spell—and with a history of kidnapping and violence—it was perfect. Apollo used some fake ID to rent the flat on that estate, and Andrea disappeared."

Originally, they thought Tony would crumble in a couple of days.

"Tinker had paid some screw to smuggle in a burner phone and get it into Tony's hands. But he wouldn't crack. And it all really turned to shit when Mike popped up at that pub and Apollo was arrested."

"Hang on. Wouldn't crack? So you really think Tony's sitting on a fortune?"

"Absolutely no doubt about it."

The lads all nodded in agreement.

"So they just hunkered down in that flat with no real plan?"

"Pretty much. Just making more rope to hang themselves with."

Tinker had controlled the narrative throughout, seemingly throwing both Apollo and Andrea under the bus at times. He had convinced them that all the negative and scandalous coverage would have more impact and help them achieve their collective goals. Presenting them as spoilt brats who had made bad decisions entertained the masses and fuelled much of the social media coverage and debate. But in reality, there was only one intended viewer: Tony.

"With Tony on a charge and then retreating into himself, it got pretty fucking dark, pretty fucking quickly."

Tinker knew he couldn't trust Andrea. If she suddenly reappeared, it wouldn't be long before she pointed the finger at him and Apollo. He wanted her dead, but neither he nor Apollo had the guts to do it.

"Andrea thought she was in control, but the tables turned, and she soon became the victim of her own scam."

"Talk about life imitating art."

"So they just kept her there, unable to trust each other, until the inevitable happened—one of them would have snapped, and two of them would have been dead."

"So Terri maybe saved their lives when she walked past?"

"Maybe."

I was never going to tell her that. Her ego was already big enough without being called a hero. Although, I was sure I wasn't alone in thinking that she'd look good in a skintight suit and a cape

I'd never seen the guys so animated. They all had a history and a story to tell. But this was pure box office. Our smoke breaks out in the yard became must-attend events. Rather than being a distraction, it actually bolstered productivity, with Sally refusing to unlock the office door if we were behind schedule.

Smiling All The Way To The Grave

I wasn't surprised to learn about Tony's death. I wasn't even surprised by the sudden and violent nature of his passing. What did surprise me was how I learned the full extent of the tragedy—through Filip, all the way over in Poland.

Tony was at the end of a line of guys waiting to be patted down and released from his training centre at the end of a shift.

Before they were allowed back onto the wings, an officer checked that all the tools in the workshop had been safely returned and locked away in a secure cabinet. A missing knife meant a full lockdown.

The guys at *The Hard Times* took lockdown in their stride. They were in an office, where they could distract themselves with work, get up from their desks, stretch their legs, speak to someone they didn't share a pad with, and—never to be underestimated—shit behind a locked door.

Oliver monitored the situation through the tiny barred window above his desk.

"Check out those poor cunts in the yard."

The rain had started coming down, and with all the gates locked, they were stuck in no-man's land, getting soaked.

"There's always someone in a worse situation."

"Too right, Harry. Look! It's that cunt Apollo. I always knew he was wet."

Apollo stood in the yard, looking thoroughly miserable.

I was surprised to see Tinker out there too. He stood by the gate leading to A Wing, his face completely blank.

"I thought he was on the VP wing."

"Not anymore. Moved to General Population last night. Couldn't stand being locked up with bloody nonces. To be honest, the lads haven't got a problem with him being an ex-screw. I mean, not many of the guys remember him, and he was trying to fuck them over, wasn't he?"

"Yeah, he's more like us than any of them. The screws, though… they bloody hate him."

According to Filip, back in the training workshop the officers were slowly and methodically searching Tony's colleagues before pushing them out into the rain—effectively a holding pen—where they would be searched again before being allowed to progress.

Tony stood quietly in line, that fixed smile still on his face.

It was only when the officers reached the man in front of him that things erupted.

"Step forward, Bogdan."

But before Bogdan could move, Tony grabbed him, pulled out the blade, and dragged the man to the floor.

With the knife pressed against his jugular, Bogdan didn't fight back. He curled up into a tight little ball, which Tony aggressively rolled around like a wrestler, grunting manically into his face before suddenly pushing him free.

Then, without hesitation, he drew the knife across his own throat and dropped to the floor.

Bogdan slipped as he tried to scramble away from the fountain of blood spurting from Tony's gargling throat. The smile never left Tony's face.

The officers could do nothing.

"He bled out like a stuck pig and was dead within a matter of seconds."

Just like Alex before him, the lads didn't talk about Tony after that.

There was a sense of sadness in the office, but it was never addressed.

It's not usual to know someone you've become fond of doing something so terrible to themselves and not react. But the lads were made of stronger stuff. I guess they'd all done and seen such terrible things that it didn't seem so strange. Perhaps they'd contemplated similar exit strategies.

It didn't bear thinking about.

But I couldn't stop thinking about it.

I tried to hold it together during the day but—and I'm not ashamed to admit it—I broke down in Gabe's car on the way home.

Gabe didn't know what to do or say, so he left me quietly sobbing while he drove.

As we arrived at my flat, I reached for my wallet, only to realise I'd left it in my locker.

"Pay me tomorrow, mate."

I'm guessing Gabe called Terri after dropping me off, because she was on the phone within seconds of me stepping into my flat.

I don't know how many of *The Hard Times* crew also broke down behind locked doors that night.

But I was damn sure none of them had a friend as good as Gabe or Terri.

Shock Jocks

There are probably worse ways to learn that your life is about to fall apart again. But hearing two overly jovial radio presenters joking about it while you're trying to digest breakfast is certainly up there.

"So, I won £100 on a scratch card yesterday, and I was wondering how I might invest that money."

"Well, I might just have the very thing for you today. Read about it in the financial pages of this morning's paper."

"Oh! What's that then?"

"How would you like to invest in a business that's recently made more than its fair share of headlines?"

"Love a business with good PR. Tell me more."

"They have connections in government that go all the way to the top. And boy, have they shaken things up recently—both locally and nationally."

"Real movers and shakers, you're saying."

"And here's the best bit."

"Go on, go on. This cash is burning a hole in my pocket."

"Their employees love working there so much, they virtually do it for free."

"There's got to be a downside?"

"Well… if you count the recent stories of staff faking a kidnap, multiple team members 'unaliving' themselves, and their connection to the downfall of a prominent government minister, I suppose you could say the company has had some issues in recent months. There's also the challenge—yes, let's call it a challenge—of working with a team of men with a body count, and I don't mean a 'sexy time' body count, in double figures."

"Hang on, hang on. All of a sudden, I'm seeing red flags."

"Do you think?"

"Yeah. I think I'd be better off investing my money in a full English somewhere."

"Ha ha! We've been talking about this all morning. *The Hard Times* newspaper—a publication that proudly boasts it's written *by offenders, for offenders*—is up for sale. And the owner, a lovely woman by the name of Bev, only wants a cool £2 million for it."

"Blimey. What an opportunity. I think I'll pass."

"Would you want to work with such a motley crew and pay £2 million for the privilege? We'll be opening up the phone lines straight after we speak to Bea, who's up there with the eye in the sky. Bea, how's the traffic looking this morning?"

"Well, I don't see too many entrepreneurs heading to North Shore Prison with bundles of cash to invest."

"Ha ha. Good one, Bea. Good one."

For Sale: One Newspaper, Slightly Used

The mood in the office couldn't have been worse.

The radio show had been piped onto the wings while the lads grabbed their breakfast. Most of the men were proud to work for *The Hard Times*—hearing themselves so publicly ridiculed was a tough pill to swallow.

Sally was particularly furious.

"Those smug, cheesy bastards. They've got no idea about the work we do in here or what we've done for the lads in North Shore—and wider society, for that matter. We've got an 80% rehabilitation rate. Nobody else can do that. And we're a *profitable* business. Doesn't cost the taxpayer a penny."

Harry looked especially sore.

"They can say what they want, we're already at the bottom of the heap. Can't get any lower than us."

"Harry! That's not like you. You've always said you felt like you were doing something good when you came to work here."

"Yeah. It just hurts to be reminded what the rest of the world thinks about you."

"What do you reckon will happen to us if they sell the paper? I don't want to re-train for a fucking job in the laundry."

"I'm sure it won't come to that, Gary. This place has no assets other than its employees, a few old computers, and a lot of goodwill. They've got to be selling it as a going concern."

Oliver's phone rang.

"Hello, newsdesk… Hey Boss! Filip wants to speak with you."

"Hey Filip. I guess you've heard the news?"

"About *The Hard Times* being for sale? Yes, Bev and I have been working on it for a few weeks now. That's why I'm calling. I was wondering—would you like to come visit me in Poland?"

"Filip, that's very sweet of you, and I'd love a little holiday, but I really don't think that's a good idea right now. Do you?"

"Oh no, not a holiday. Strictly business. I insist. I've spoken to Bev—she agrees it's a good idea. I've booked flights for you, flying out of East Midlands next week. Your friend Gabe can take you to the airport. It's all arranged. I'll email your tickets and hotel details now."

"Do I have a choice?"

"You always have a choice, Euan. It's just about knowing what's good for you. I'll see you next week."

I turned to Sally.

"Didn't I *used* to be Filip's boss?"

"I think so."

"It's funny, I don't remember getting the memo about his sudden promotion."

I had no idea what was going to happen at work—and now I'd somehow been booked onto a city break to Warsaw with a Polish drug mule cosplaying as Alan bloody Sugar.

"Sally, tell me… does high blood pressure have any symptoms?"

"I'm not sure. How do you feel?"

"Like my head's about to explode."

"Yep. That could be one of them."

A One-Way Ticket to Chaos

Gabe was full of the joys.

"I love an airport run. £200 in my back pocket. I might just take the rest of the day off. So, where are you heading again?"

"Poland."

"Poland? Bloody hell. Well, at least you'll have an empty flight going over there."

"How do you work that out?"

"Well, they're all too bloody busy coming over here and stealing our jobs, aren't they? Bloody Nige'll stop 'em when we vote them out."

Good old Gabe. You could always rely on him to revert to stereotype when you needed reassurance that the world wasn't spinning too fast.

Gabe was wrong. The flight was packed.

This was no holiday flight. The bulk of the passengers looked like manual workers—farmhands, factory labourers. Hard as nails and, for the most part, drunk as fuck.

I was squashed between two huge Polish men in the middle seat. They were speaking to each other and laughing loudly.

"You don't speak Polish?" one of them asked.

"No, just English, I'm afraid."

"Don't be afraid. I too was afraid of flying, but I have the answer."

"Oh, I'm not afraid of—"

"I drink."

He pulled a bottle of vodka and three plastic glasses from his hand luggage.

"Do you drink?"

"Well, it's a bit—"

"You drink!"

"What the hell. It would be rude not to."

The pilot interrupted our little vodka party to make an announcement.

"We're just waiting on two more passengers to join us, and then we'll get the doors shut and be on our way."

Two men boarded the flight through the rear door. One was dressed smartly in a black pullover, trousers, and a freshly pressed shirt. The other looked like he'd just crawled off The Beaches Estate in tracky bottoms and a Sports Direct top.

They were handcuffed, which made getting into their seats difficult.

"I'm going to take these off now. Are you going to behave?"

"I'm looking forward to going home. There won't be any trouble."

"Good. We'll get you there. There'll be a bit of admin at the airport, and if everything checks out, you'll be good to go this afternoon."

My neighbour nudged me heavily in the ribs, spilling my vodka.

"Someone's been a naughty boy."

Without being prompted, my glass was topped up again. This flight was going to be a nightmare.

No sooner had we taken off than my drinking companion was asleep, his head on my shoulder, snoring loudly.

At least now I might have a chance of arriving at my destination sober.

An Offer I Couldn't Refuse

Filip had arranged for a taxi to take me into the city centre. I don't know much about cars, but this one was twice the size and three times as clean as Gabe's. The driver was also impressive—suited and booted, clean-shaven, and speaking better English than most of the locals I'd come across in Cragsholme.

As we pulled up outside the Warsaw Marriott, I suddenly realised I didn't have any zloty.

"I'm going to have to find a cash machine, mate. I've got no money."

"No problem, sir. I take cards."

The driver flashed a card reader at me.

I couldn't wait to tell Gabe about this. He would have been disgusted. For Gabe, cash was king and the only acceptable way to pay for a ride in his car. Imagine a *"third-world country"* like Poland being so progressive.

Filip met me in the reception. He looked great.

"Nice threads."

I was so used to seeing him in that grey, prison-issue jogging suit.

"Thank you. I'm a businessman now. I like to look the part."

The hotel had a business centre where Filip had set up shop.

"It's only temporary, but it will do for the time being."

"Wow. It's a bit nicer than *The Hard Times* office at North Shore."

"The restaurant is also better. You should try the *rosół*—it's a nice chicken soup, just like my grandmother used to make."

"Sounds nice. I'll give it a try. But I'm not here to talk about soup. What's going on, Filip?"

"Good. I'm glad you want to get down to business. As you know, *The Hard Times* is for sale, and Bev has instructed me to speak with interested parties. So, I'll cut to the chase. I want you to buy it."

I laughed.

"It's not a joke, Euan. I—I mean *we*—really do think you should buy it."

"Look, mate, I don't know who you think I am, but I haven't got a spare two quid at the moment, let alone two million."

"Ah, Euan, about that price tag... that was fake news. A typo. Bev is actually asking for £2.5 million."

"It might as well be £250 million. I haven't got it. So, if that's the reason why you've dragged me over here, it's been a waste of time. I mean, really, Filip—this could have been an email or a phone call. I've got a paper to get out, and if you don't mind me saying, this has been a complete waste of time."

"What if I told you I could lend you the money?"

"I'd ask you where you got the money from. You've just got out of jail, and I know how much Bev is paying you."

"This has nothing to do with my little salary at *The Hard Times*. I have connections, and *that* is why this conversation couldn't be an email or a phone call."

Okay, now I was worried.

I might have spent the best part of a year sharing an office with violent criminals, but there was always a degree of separation between my world and theirs. Now, it looked like I was being propositioned to effectively join their ranks.

There was a knock at the door.

"Ah, he's here. Come in, Bogdan. You look fucking terrible."

It was the young man from the plane.

The pair of them hugged and spoke in Polish for what felt like an eternity.

"I'm sorry, we're being very rude. You might know Bogdan. No? He was my cellmate in North Shore. We became very close friends. But he's had quite a day—I can certainly appreciate that. His first day of freedom, back home at last.

"We're keen to sort this business out, but first, he needs to get cleaned up and wash that prison smell off. Why don't you check into your room, and we'll meet up for dinner tonight?"

As soon as I was behind my hotel room door, I called Bev. From the dial tone, I guessed she was in Spain.

"What the fuck is going on, Bev?"

"What do you mean?"

"Filip wants me to buy *The Hard Times*."

"Don't you want to buy *The Hard Times*?"

"Where's the money coming from?"

"I think you already know the answer to that question."

"Jesus, Bev—you're as bent as half the bastards in that prison."

"We're all living in *hard times*, Euan. I'd have thought you'd have figured that out by now. My time at *The Hard Times* is over. Listen to Filip—he has a solution to all of our problems."

Three Little Words

"Tony told you, didn't he?"

Bogdan glanced at Filip, seeking approval to continue. Filip nodded.

"About his money? Yes. Just before he cut his throat and bled out on the floor."

"Why you?"

"I have no idea. I'd never even spoken to him before. I just thought he was crazy."

"What did he tell you?"

"Just three words, over and over again."

"Three words? What three words?"

"Just three random words. It didn't make any sense at the time, but when a man takes his life after whispering three words into your ear, you remember them."

"What three words?"

"It doesn't matter anymore. We worked it out."

"It was a puzzle?"

"No, it's a website. Actually, an app. Filip told me when he was delivering packages, they would use it to find drop-off and collection points. You can pinpoint any place on earth using just three words.

"I told my friends, and what do you know? Tony's three words led them to a location where they found—well, let's just say—a hell of a lot of money."

Filip interrupted.

"Of course, they spent some of that money, but do you know how hard it is to spend cash these days? We lost a lot of it getting it clean and feeding it into the banking system. But that gave us some more ideas, which we can discuss later."

"Hang on. When did you do all this?"

"Oh, we've been working on it for quite a while—even when Bogdan was back in North Shore. That's the beautiful thing about speaking Polish. The screws and the other guys on the wing had no idea what we were talking about. The best secrets are always hidden in plain sight."

"Like your television star Jimmy Savile."

"No, Bogdan. That is not a good example."

"So, where is the cash now?"

"It's in a bank account in Bermuda. Just waiting to be paid out to you as a loan via a holding company. They pay you, you pay Bev, I get a small commission, and everyone is happy."

I shook my head.

"I can see you're still not convinced. We'll speak more about this tomorrow. Perhaps you'll see things differently after you've slept on it.

"But before you sleep on it, we need to show you how we party in Warsaw."

I don't know if you've ever been on a night out you didn't want to go on—with two blokes who had just been released from prison and didn't seem to be short of cash.

Three words came to mind: *Horrible, Degrading, Shit.*

As for sleeping on Filip's business proposal, that didn't happen either.

A Deal with the Devil

"Euan, it's a good business. Let's put aside how you get your hands on it. It's a bloody good business."

Filip then broke down all the outgoings and income.

"Half of the money comes in from the government, NGOs, and charities. They're not tracking ROI or anything like that. Doesn't matter if the advertising works or not. They just keep spending, because if they don't, their budgets get cut—and nobody wants that."

"Cynical."

"Maybe. But it's true. It's a licence to print money. Then there's the outgoings. It costs nothing to print a few thousand newspapers, the rent is low, and you know how little you can pay your staff. What's the average? Ten quid a week?"

"Yep. Nobody's getting rich at *The Hard Times*."

"We can."

Filip then laid out his plans for growing the business.

"We don't really want you to do anything differently. But we may occasionally ask you to raise some invoices for additional services."

"What kind of services?"

"Editorial services, public relations, website design, SEO."

"We don't do any of that."

"And we're not going to start. This will all be outsourced to other companies Bogdan and I are working with."

"Genuine companies?"

"Maybe. Maybe not. It's not important."

It suddenly dawned on me.

"So basically, you're asking me to help you launder more money?"

"Like I said, it's a very good business. Lots of people are looking for this service."

"I don't know…"

Filip's smile faded.

"Listen, we need an answer. And I don't need to remind you—given the information we've shared—well, let's just say we'd be very upset if your answer was *no*."

There it was. The threat.

"Our lawyer will be with us tomorrow. We'll sign the paperwork and get the ball rolling. Yes?"

I nodded, trying to appear noncommittal.

"Good. Our lawyer's a good guy. You can trust him."

I needed to speak to someone I actually *could* trust—but they were few and far between. I wouldn't drag Sally into this. Risking her prison service pension wasn't an option.

That left Terri.

But with Filip and Bogdan constantly watching me, making that call was going to be difficult.

"Then it's agreed. Tomorrow, we sign the deal and become business partners. Tonight, we drink. Yes?"

Luckily for me, they got slopey when they drank. And they *loved* to drink.

We were in yet another girlie bar. They were teasing me for not wanting to take one of the girls to a private room.

"Filip, I think he might be gay," Bogdan jeered.

"Funny little gay Englishman."

"What about her, Euan? You like her?"

A girl in towering heels handed me a laminated menu of *services*.

"This is more than a dance club, isn't it?"

"It's on the company."

I saw my opportunity.

I followed the girl to a private room.

"I'm Alina," she purred. "You want to have some fun with me tonight? What would you like me to do?"

"Well… this might be a little unusual, but do you mind if I phone my girlfriend?"

Terri found the situation *hilarious*.

"So, let me get this straight. You're phoning me from a brothel in Poland to tell me your boss is a crook, and you've been embroiled in an international money-laundering scheme?"

"That's about it in a nutshell."

"Bloody hell. Beats a night out with Daisy in The Beaches."

"Listen, what should I do?"

"Hang on. You told her I was your girlfriend?"

"Yeah. Sorry about that. It just sounded like the right thing to say."

"That poor girl. She turns up to work, half-naked, throws herself at you, and all you want to do is talk to *me*? She must be devastated."

"She's having a fag. I think she's glad of the break."

"You really know how to treat a girl."

"Terri. I've already been in here way too long. What should I do?"

"I think you should do it."

"Pardon?"

"I said I think you should do it. And I'll help."

Alina ruffled my hair and unbuttoned the top three buttons of my shirt. I handed her 400 zloty for her trouble.

Filip and Bogdan *cheered* when I emerged from the room.

"Fifteen minutes!" Filip roared. "Bogdan said you'd only manage two."

"Get the drinks in, lads. I'm in."

Welcome Home

The lawyer was incredibly efficient.

I was certain he knew the operation was bent, but he carefully went through all the documents, making sure I understood exactly what I was signing.

"See? I told you that you could trust him. This is a professional operation," Filip said with a smug grin.

With the paperwork complete, Filip called me a taxi, and I headed straight to the airport.

The flight back was far more civilised than the one on the way over. I had three seats to myself and even managed to get some much-needed sleep. The journey was smooth, but the landing came with a bit of a bump—perhaps a forewarning of what was to come.

As I disembarked, a policeman stepped into my path.

"May I see your passport, sir?"

I handed it over.

"And where have you been flying from today, sir?"

"Er… Poland. You literally just saw me get off the plane."

"No need for that, sir. We're only doing our job."

The officer spoke briefly into his radio before turning back to me.

"We'd like you to come with us, sir. We have a few more questions."

"Am I under arrest?"

"Not yet, sir. Not yet."

I was taken to the airport police station, where they interrogated me further before finally reading me my rights.

"Under the *Proceeds of Crime Act 2002*, it is an offence to acquire, use, or possess criminal property if the person knows or suspects it represents criminal proceeds. Therefore, we'll be arresting you today for possession of criminal property.

You do not have to say anything, but it may harm your defence if you do not mention, when questioned, something which you later rely on in court. Anything you do say may be given in evidence."

"Fuck."

I'd been an international criminal for less than a day, and I was already behind bars.

The question is, who dobbed me in? Surely not Terri? It could have only been her.

In hindsight, thank God she did.

Red Carpets and Redemption

Sixteen months after my arrest, I was walking along a red carpet outside the Southbank Centre in London.

"You look nice, Terri."

"Why, thank you, Euan. You look kind of tired and awkward."

She was right. I had a unique ability to look scruffy in a tuxedo.

"Are you feeling lucky?"

"No such thing as luck, Euan. We deserve this."

"Terri! Who are you wearing?"

"It's Stella McCartney. Lush, isn't it? Hey, did you know her dad was in a band called The Beatles? I was today years old when I found out."

"Did you really just say that?"

"Yeah. I like winding them up."

"That'll be in all the papers tomorrow."

"Good job nobody reads them anymore then, isn't it?"

She laughed playfully, but she knew she was right.

We took our seats in the auditorium.

It was one of the dullest events I'd ever attended. I think I lost the will to live somewhere between the nominations for *Best Extreme Minimalist Living Podcast* and some other pretentious and probably fake lifestyle category. I was pretty sure none of the nominees had ever lived in a prison cell overlooking Cragsholme Beach.

Terri nudged me.

"Are you still awake? We're up next."

A photo of Terri standing in front of *The Beaches Inn* was projected onto the screen at the back of the stage.

"I'm sure this young lady needs no introduction to most of the people in the room tonight. She's a rising global star—not just in the world of social media and podcasting but across the broader media landscape."

"Are you blushing?"

"Nah, I'm loving it. He ain't saying anything I don't already know."

"Legions of fans know her on YouTube as *Terri Talks*. But she's evolved. And tonight, we're celebrating her incredible success in what is, dare I say, perhaps the most impactful piece of investigative journalism in the past twelve months."

"Fucking hell, Terri. How's that ego of yours doing?"

She was beaming from ear to ear.

"Terri's podcast, *Living Hard Times*, not only exposed a significant money laundering operation—an international gang smuggling millions of pounds of drugs across Europe into the UK—it also uncovered widespread corruption in the British prison system.

She revealed how individuals cynically exploited cheap prison labour to line their pockets while publicly presenting themselves as advocates of reform. If you've been following the news, you'll know that some of those people have recently embarked on their own experience of life behind bars."

"That'll be Bev, then."

"Well, at least she's got Andrea for company."

"Terri also shed light on how completely innocent individuals were coerced into assisting these criminal operations and suffered the consequences. One such man is with us today. I'm pleased to say that not only have all charges against him been dropped, but he was recently invited to consult with the Home Office on how businesses can better support rehabilitation in the prison system.

Euan—where are you, young man?"

"Ha! *Young man*! He must have you mistaken for someone else."

I stood up, raised my hand, and was completely taken aback by the round of applause.

"Terri could have stopped there. But she didn't. She went on to highlight the vital work organisations like *The Hard Times* do in rehabilitating offenders, proving the point that we should never throw the baby out with the bathwater just because of a few bad eggs. There is always light in the darkest of times—if you look for it."

The host moved to the side of the stage, and a familiar face appeared on screen.

"W-working at *The Hard Times* has g-given me a sense of pride in e-everything I-I-I do."

"Mike's stammer is getting so much better."

"Well, he's becoming a more confident man."

"I don't know what I did to deserve the k-kindness people like Euan have sh-shown me over the y-years, but it's ch-changed my perspective on life. I've not always been p-perfect. I've done some terrible things. But Euan has always accepted me at face value, w-w-warts and all.

His mentorship h-has allowed me to move on in l-life. And now, I'm incredibly p-proud to call myself the new editor of *The Hard Times*."

Terri squeezed my arm.

"Are you crying?"

"Terri's belief in Euan and his w-work at *The Hard Times*, and her subsequent podcast, was instrumental in en-ensuring justice was done. A-as a former career crim-criminal, I never thought I'd say that.

Her podcast not only s-s-saved Euan from p-prosecution—it secured m-my future. I-I have another c-couple of years remaining on my sentence, b-but I know that there are o-other people at the p-paper ready to rise to the c-challenge Euan has set.

When you believe in p-people, they might just surprise you. I'm so g-g-glad that T-Terri believed in this project—and in Euan.

Th-thank you."

The entire room rose to its feet, applauding.

I looked back at the audience and just caught sight of Sally, looking fabulous in a red dress—though I was pretty sure she still had a pair of Doc Martens on her feet. Standing next to her was Oliver, clearly enjoying his first weekend release.

I was glad to see his five-year plan was moving forward at pace.

"Before we leave tonight, we need to get a photo of those two together. I never thought I'd see the day Oliver wore a tux. Even if he is fit to burst out of it. Must have bought it from the kids' department."

"Well, it's hard to dress a man on a prison job salary when he's got guns like Oliver."

"Don't you start fancying my old colleagues. We know where that gets people."

Terri took to the stage like a mini explosion. For once, she wasn't composed. She was at a loss for words.

"You might know me as *Terri Talks*, but today, I'm not talking. Other than to say—thank you.

Thank you to Euan for inviting me into his world and letting me rescue him."

Scattered laugher and applause.

"And by the way, for everyone saying Euan's my boyfriend—he isn't.

More laughter.

"What about Mike? We're so proud."

A few cheers from the crowd.

"What I'm trying to say is—believe in yourself and in other people, and we might just change the world. This little podcast has certainly changed mine."

She paused for a moment, stepping back from the mic.

"I don't know if I'm allowed to say this yet, but… Netflix wants to turn my little podcast into a three-part documentary. I might be in trouble for telling you that. Oh well. Laters, haters."

A New Broom (Mop)

Sally met me at the prison reception.

"You never did get your own keychain and belt, did you?"

"I never really wanted the responsibility."

"Ha. And look at you now, coming into HMP North Shore to meet the new Minister of State for Prisons. You've gone up in the world."

"You taught me everything I know, Sally."

"I'm sure. You always were full of crap."

"No, I mean it. Patience, compassion—um, patience. Did I ever tell you that you were really patient? No, seriously, you showed me how to treat people right, even if the rest of the world is afraid of them or wants to hate them. The success of *The Hard Times* project wasn't down to Bev, for all her sins, or me. It was all down to you and the relationships you built with the lads."

"Now you really are just speaking shit. Come on, the Minister is waiting for us."

The new Minister was standing in the yard with the Governor and Mike.

"How is he still here?" I asked.

"The Governor? He's only got a few weeks to go before he retires and hits the golf course. I think they've turned a blind eye to his naivety and incompetence in the hope of keeping it out of the papers. God knows HMP North Shore has had its fair share of column inches. You've had one or two yourself."

"Hello, Euan. Nice to see you again, Sally. I don't believe in standing on ceremony, so please call me Eric. Now, Mike has been telling me about all the great things you've been doing here, but Sally insists that I'll never truly understand the workings of a prison until I visit the lads on the wing. It's where she said they do their real hard time. So, what are we waiting for? Let's go."

I'm glad to say that I never got used to walking onto a prison wing. After I was arrested and subsequently charged, I was granted bail and only had to suffer the indignity of wearing a tag until Terri cleared my name.

The smell still sickened me. The noise of every footstep, key turning, and door opening before being slammed shut echoed around the almost empty wing, almost instantly bringing on a migraine.

"I thought they would have fixed this place up before the Minister arrived."

The mismatched chairs, empty TV bracket, and pool table with ripped felt—adding to the issue of no balls or cues—just highlighted the fact that when things get broken in North Shore, they stay broken. A perfect metaphor for the Minister's visit.

"Now then, who have we got here?"

A man stood leaning on a mop, surveying the situation. His face was full of disgust. He clearly felt his job was beneath him and wasn't going to play the part of a performing monkey just because we had a VIP visitor.

"That's Gypo. He's supposed to be working, keeping the wing neat and tidy."

"Gypo. That is an unusual name."

The Minister lowered his voice. "Is he from the travelling community? I understand they make up a significant portion of the prison population, disproportionately so compared to their numbers in general society."

"Ha ha. No, he's not a traveller, unless they've packed up and set up camp on Fleet Street. No, that's just what the lads call him. His real name is Tinker. Used to be a journalist before he wound up in here."

"Tinker, is it? I remember him now. Surely he'd be a good fit for a job on *The Hard Times*. What's he doing mopping floors?"

"W-we only work w-with p-people we can trust, Sir. Nobody in here t-trusts him. Not us on *The H-Hard Times*. Not the screws. Besides, h-he might be s-shit at mopping floors, but h-he was an even w-worse journalist."

"Quite. I love how you men tell it as it is. No filter. And what about that lad over there polishing the phones?"

"That's Apollo. He doesn't cause us any problems. If anything, he needs looking after. People take advantage of him. Actually, you might have heard of him as well.."

"Ah yes. Apollo. Son of Zeus and Leto. Known for his numerous love affairs, some of which resulted in tragic outcomes."

Sally looked confused. "No. I'm sorry, Sir. I think you are mistaken. His mum's name is Bev. Didn't know his dad was Greek. Although, I guess that makes sense. Everything else checks out, though."

Printed in Dunstable, United Kingdom

64945521R00139